Justin Richards

BIG FINISH

Also available in this series:

Professor Bernice Summerfield and the Dead Men Diaries
ISBN 1-903654-04-1

Published by Big Finish Productions Ltd,
PO Box 1127
Maidenhead SL6 3LW

www.bernicesummerfield.com

Range editors: Gary Russell & Jacqueline Rayner
Managing Editor: Jason Haigh-Ellery

First published November 2000

ISBN 1–903654–04–1

Cover art by Carolyn Edwards © 2000
Logo designed by Paul Vyse

Printed and bound in Great Britain by Biddles Ltd
www.biddles.co.uk

For Gary – because he cares about Benny more than any of us.
For Jac – because she understands Benny better than any of us.
For my Mum – because she keeps dropping hints.
And for Alison, Julian and Christian – because...

Welcome to the Braxiatel Collection

The Greatest Collection in the Known Universe

Please note that this is a working document and is not yet approved for public release. Since the Collection is still under construction, information is subject to change.Make sure you have the latest copy.

Broderick Naismith (Chief Publicity Relations Officer)

Overview: What is the Braxiatel Collection?

Owned and managed by Irving Braxiatel himself, the Braxiatel Collection is arguably the finest and most extensive collection in the known universe. Collection of what? is an invalid question. It is a collection of everything. The various departments of the Braxiatel Collection house antique artefacts, literature, playscripts, recordings of events and people and performances, geological specimens, software and hardware of days gone by Imagine the combined collections of every museum, gallery and archive you can think of and you have an idea of perhaps one tenth of the contents of the Braxiatel Collection.

It is rumoured that Braxiatel has a whole gallery devoted to Deauxob of Glanatanus; that Howard Carter's original notebooks from the Tutankhamen expedition have a small space on a long shelf in the Archaeology Archives. Somewhere in a dust-covered specimen cabinet, it is suggested that Braxiatel has a complete manuscript (some even say the original manuscript) of Stanoff Osterling's lost play *The Good Soldiers*.

These claims — and countless others — are of course outrageous. But once you have been privileged enough to visit the Collection, like those who have come before, you will find it easy to believe them all.

A permanent home for the Braxiatel Collection is currently under construction on a small planetoid formerly designated KS-159. The planetoid is now known as The Braxiatel Collection. Gravity, you will be pleased to note, is kept at 1.0 Earth Normal (1EN).

There is a rumour that Irving Braxiatel won the planetoid at cards on Vega Station. Like most rumours about Braxiatel himself, this is entirely true.

One rumour that has never been substantiated, however, is that the fabled Oracle of the Lost is situated on the planetoid. It is said that Braxiatel has preserved the excavated ruins of the Temple of the Lost within one of the outbuildings — possibly the Small Trianon (which is out of bounds to all visitors).

Visiting the Braxiatel Collection
Once the Collection's permanent home is complete, then it may be opened to the general public. But for the foreseeable future, visitors are accepted by personal (and privileged) invitation only.

To qualify for a personal invitation to the Braxiatel Collection you will probably fall into one of the following categories:

Noted academic from a long-established institution of good repute.

Someone who has been able to make a donation to the Collection in the past, or who has something to offer now.

Someone substantially involved in one of the many research missions throughout space sponsored directly by the Braxiatel Collection. (Note that the only condition attached to such a grant should it be forthcoming is that the findings — both theories and raw data — be returned for storage at the Braxiatel Collection.)

Security
Your plasti-disc invitation is also your security pass for the Braxiatel Collection. Do not lose it.

The disc is a small round piece of pink plastic, about two imperial inches in diameter. The disc is keyed to your personal bio-emissions, so you cannot give it to someone else, and you can only use your own disc. Having your disc in close proximity to your body (in a pocket or handbag, for example) iis sufficient for recognition purposes. Note that the disc also knows your security clearance level, so will not open doors to areas where you are not permitted access. If you should lose your plasti-disc, you will need to apply to Ms Jones (Admin Facility) for a replacement.

When You Arrive

You will arrive at the Braxiatel Collection's Reception Area. Here your plasti-disc invitation will be checked (as it was before boarding the shuttle that brought you to the Collection) by a Receptionist-cum-Security Officer. You will then be directed to local transportation for the main Collection.

But spare a moment when you arrive to admire the view through the huge picture window opposite the Reception Desk. This gives a view out over the ornamental gardens towards the Mansionhouse — the main building (and Irving Braxiatel's private residence). Note in particular the terraces stretching into the distance — the curvature of the planetoid is such that they seem to drop away ever steeper until they disappear from sight, the sculptured waterfalls spraying their last cascades out over the edge of the world.

The Mansionhouse and its grounds have been based on the ancient Earth (local ref: France) Palace of Versailles. But it is commonly acknowledged that if Louis XIV could have seen what Braxiatel has accomplished he would have sacked his architects and landscapers and started again.

Transportation

Depending on which department you are visiting, or if you want to check into your accommodation in 'The Hamlet' at the edge of the gardens, you have a choice of transports.

The Braxiatel planetoid is not big. Its circumference is approximately ten miles, and so it is possible to walk to any location as it is only a maximum of five miles away. Some people enjoy the walk out of the back entrance to the Mansionhouse, round the entire planetoid in a straight line, and arriving back at the main entrance.

But for those who do not have the time or the inclination, there are horse-and-carriages available (for main routes only), or you can ride in one of the state of the art Ormand-Seltec Flyers. You will spot them on their designated pads. Be careful to avoid the overhead rotors when boarding.

Finding your way Around

NB: Please note that the Braxiatel Collection is still being constructed. The Mansionhouse is virtually complete, as are some of the outbuildings, but internal design and furbishment continues even in these. Similarly, the land is terraformed and the grounds are mapped out, but there is still much to be done. You will please keep to designated areas and well away from construction and landscaping areas.

Should you require more information, please apply to Ms Jones who will put you in touch either with Adrian Wall (construction) or Mister Crofton (grounds). Your help and understanding is appreciated.

Departments

There are so many departments at the Braxiatel Collection that it would take too much space to list them all. Up-to-date, online listings are available at the spaceport and in your accommodation. Alternatively, please ask any member of the Collection s staff for directions.

The Hamlet

The Hamlet is a small 'village' of accommodation situated on the banks of the Great Trianon Lake, three miles north east (seven miles south east) of the Mansionhouse. This is where you will stay if your invitation extends overnight (there is a day/night cycle corresponding to Earth Normal). You will find that the Hamlet is a 'fairytale' collection of cottages. Most of these cottages are thatched and are comprised of two storeys. A notable exception is the Mill which has its own ornamental waterwheel (or rather, it will have when it's finished and the teething problems with the gravimetric induction motor are sorted out). Restaurant facilites are available in the Dairy and there is a wine bar, The Caretaker's Cottage which offers an assortment of beers, wines, liqueurs, milk shakes and bar snacks. Other facilities are under construction.

The Mansionhouse

The Mansionhouse is modelled on the main Chateau of the Palace of Versailles. It contains several of the Collection's departments (see above). Aside from these departments, the Mansionhouse is not generally accessible to visitors and includes the private accommodation of Irving Braxiatel and his personal staff.

The Grand Trianon

The Grand Trianon is equidistant from the Mansionhouse both to north and south. It is an impressive, largely rectangular building of stone and marble with a pillared frontage. The pillars are veined red marble.

The Small Trianon

The Small Trianon is off-limits to all visitors. Attempted entry is strictly forbidden.

The Great Stables and the Small Stables

Still under construction. Details to follow when available.

The Grounds and Gardens

The design of the smaller buildings in the grounds (such as the Summer-House in the Garden of Whispers) is by the famous Dupok, who created holographic models of all the buildings for the construction teams to work from. It is obviously impractical to describe the entire grounds and gardens, especially as much is still being landscaped. You will find a map of the completed areas in your accommodation.

1
Matinee Performance

His credentials were as false as his hand. His invitation card gave his name as Dr Josiah Vanderbilt and he looked more like 37 than 87. Which was fine, because a carefully placed scuff mark made the '8' look like a '3' and the data integrity was equally smudged.

'Welcome to the Braxiatel Collection,' he murmured to himself as he folded the thin brochure and returned it to his inside jacket pocket. For the sake of appearance rather than out of interest he did indeed spare a glance at the view from the huge picture window opposite the Reception Desk. It was certainly as impressive as the brochure suggested. It left him cold, he had seen so many things.

Ahead of him, the queue of about a dozen passengers from the shuttle was passing through a security gate. He could see each in turn struggling to understand the printed instructions, then sliding the small plastic security clearance disc that came with their invitation into a reader set into the side of the gate. People further down the queue were craning to see what those at the front were doing.

'Welcome to Braxiatel, Dr Vanderbilt,' flashed up on the gate's small display screen when he slid in his disc. He allowed himself the slightest exhalation of relief as the gate opened for him, and then he was through.

'It's quite a privilege you know,' an elderly woman with a thin face and pale blue hair told him as he emerged into the sunlight. Most of the other passengers Vanderbilt saw were heading towards a flyer that squatted lazily on its landing pad. He did not answer the woman, and she kept walking, still talking, oblivious to the fact that he had stopped.

'I'm looking forward to the fireworks most, I think.' Her voice floated back to him, shrill on the still air. 'And meeting Irving Braxiatel himself of course. I hear that – oh!' She broke off, realising at last that she was alone.

He stifled a smile and looked away, pretending he had not heard. Feigning indifference.

On the back of the leaflet was a small map of the grounds. He had memorised it at a glance, and now he set off through the ornamental gardens towards the Hamlet. Across a sea of low hedges and flowering shrubs he could see the square magnificence of the Mansionhouse – Braxiatel's residence and the hub of the Collection. It was exactly as he had imagined from the briefing and the brochure. Only far bigger. One side of it was covered with a spider's web of scaffolding. Within the web he could see that several of the windows were gaping holes, the stonework and balustrades unfinished.

The grounds also seemed to be a mixture of the completed and the unfinished. They too seemed more extensive than he had anticipated. He knew to within a tenth of a kilometre the circumference of the small planet, yet the walk seemed to take longer than he had imagined. And despite his indifference, despite the terrible things he had seen in the course of his career, he found himself slowly but surely drawn into the splendour of the place. By the time he started down the Avenue of Fountains he was actually enjoying the walk. His head was clear, the air was cool and fresh, the views were inspiring, and for the first time in years he felt at one with his world. With a mixture of shock, surprise and amusement he found that he was humming quietly.

Vanderbilt paused for a moment, perhaps halfway down the avenue, and turned to look back at the Mansionhouse behind him. Whatever else he might have done, he thought, Braxiatel had got this right. It was impossible now not to feel caught up in the splendour and serenity of the place.

Turning back, he could make out the low form of the Grand Trianon ahead of him, at the end of the wide avenue. The stone and marble of the frontage caught the enhanced light of the sun, and he raised a hand to shield his eyes. At regular intervals all along the sides of the avenue there were fountains. He examined them as he continued, and saw that despite what he had originally thought, they were not all identical.

Actually, it was fascinating. Each of the fountains in the avenue looked the same from any point in the avenue. But when you got close enough to see through the curtain of water that cascaded down around the central column, you could see that each was different from the last. So far as he could tell, no two designs were repeated.

Pausing to look at one of the fountains, he found that there was a small plaque on the base. 'Cherubs' it read, and he could see now the small rounded figures that formed the central column, their tiny wings seemingly insufficient to defy the Earth-normal gravity. Moving along, the next fountain was 'Angels', the central column, masked by cascading water, featuring larger, more elegant figures this time.

Before long he found himself at the end of the avenue. The final fountain on one side seemed to be an uncarved pillar. He peered closely into the white water, shading his eyes from the glare off the shining frontage of the Grand Trianon. The stone seemed to be left exactly as it was when it was positioned, still waiting for the sculptor's chisel. His immediate assumption was that one day it would be a statue like the others – bird, beast, man, creature... Here, he thought, was a part of the grounds that was still not completed. He had seen enough evidence of work in progress both on the buildings and the grounds.

But then he caught sight of the plaque on the base of the unformed fountain. He glanced again at the unformed stone; the potential; the real statue still hidden within the uncarved block. He nodded slowly as he understood.

This fountain was called 'Future'.

The first visitors had only arrived today, so there still weren't many other people about. Which was why Professor Bernice Summerfield paid particular attention to the figure she saw making its way down the Avenue of Fountains. She was pleased to see that he seemed impressed and interested. He paused and looked and nodded and moved on.

Not that she was at all interested really, but she could see that he was tall and slim. He looked to be about Benny's own age, maybe a shade younger. Most of all she was not at all interested to notice his finely-chiselled features and the strikingly blond hair that was cut short on his head. His movements were measured and deliberate, yet at the same time there was a sense of 'cat' about him.

Benny knew a lot about cats. Most of all she knew that if she didn't find her own tabby tomcat Wolsey before long she would let him go without his afternoon treat of Freda's Fish Fancies. She wouldn't normally be bothered, except that if she wasn't busy looking for Wolsey she might find herself roped in to help with preparing the evening's celebrations.

Benny had another reason to stay outside, but she'd already decided not to worry about that until she had to. Motivated by the thought of putting off the moment as much as by concern for Wolsey, she followed the blond man down the Avenue and towards the Garden of Whispers.

As Benny entered the garden, the man was just visible – rounding the Summer-House and making his way up the grassy hill towards the path to the Hamlet. Somehow that made her feel annoyed. Well, perhaps not annoyed, but definitely miffed that he had not paused to enjoy the beauty of the place. Whoever he might be.

For her part, Benny was always overawed by the Garden of Whispers, no matter how often she visited it. Without doubt it was one of the most impressive areas of the grounds. The centrepiece was a small lake over which willows wept and oak trees towered. A perfect lawn stretched beyond the trees, bounded by the central driveway to one side and high hedges backing on to the parterres of the Small Trianon on the other.

There were statues positioned throughout the garden – human figures in classical dress, or often undress. Several lined up along the hedge, facing back towards the Mansionhouse, the roof of which Benny could just see gleaming above the foreshortened horizon.

At the far side of the lake from her, raised on a vantage point stood the Summer-House. Three shallow steps led up into it. Stone caryatids rising to the domed roof served as the only walls. Inside the building, even from across the lake, she could make out another figure posed and immobile, as if some of the statuary that hid amongst the trees had crept inside to admire the view.

The whispers were audible as soon as she started across the lawn. As if the statues were exchanging secret messages behind and around her. Knowing that it was merely the breeze picking its way through the willow trees and playing on the lake's surface did nothing to lessen the magic. Not a real breeze of course. In a sense, nothing on Braxiatel was real.

Except, Benny thought with a smile, Mister Crofton.

The head groundsman was working on the edge of the lawn beside the Summer-House, clipping the grass back from the border of a flower bed. As ever, the man was absorbed in his work – in his garden. Either he did not notice Benny's approach or he simply did not care to remark it until she was between him and the wheelbarrow. He was a short, stocky man. Even when he straightened up and wiped the sweat from his lined brow with a glistening forearm he barely came up to Benny's shoulders.

He nodded, and a strand of his thinning grey hair that had been stuck across his balding pate with perspiration broke free and flopped down the side of his weather-beaten face. He brushed it away without apparent irritation. 'Professor,' he acknowledged, his voice accented and rustic.

'Mister Crofton,' she returned with a nod. 'How are the gardens today?'

'All the better for you asking, Professor. Thank you.'

She grinned at him. 'You can call me Benny, you know,' she told him, not for the first time. She knew he wouldn't.

13

'Here to admire the view?' he asked, stooping to his work again.

'My last chance this millennium.' She gave a short laugh. 'Well, depending on when you think the millennium actually finishes.'

She crouched down beside him, watching him tease something that looked like a thistle out of the soil. The thistle's roots thrashed and tore at his gloves as Mister Crofton yanked it free. He gave it a thump on the grass, and the movement subsided. Then he tossed it past Benny towards the wheelbarrow.

'Which school do you subscribe to?' Benny asked as she straightened up again. 'The first day of 2600? Or 2601?'

'I'm not sure it really matters, does it?' he replied without looking up. 'One day is pretty much like another. Especially here.'

'Hmm,' Benny said. 'So we won't be seeing you at the big party tonight then.'

Mister Crofton smiled. 'Likely not,' he conceded. 'Mr Braxiatel tells me that there are forty-seven statues in this garden altogether. I haven't counted them, but I expect he's right.' He teased out another weed, this one less violently opposed to the eviction than the last, and examined it carefully. 'He usually is.'

'I know. Infuriating isn't it.'

'He says you can see them all from the Summer-House,' Mister Crofton went on. 'But I haven't got time to stand there and count them.'

'Well who has?' Benny asked. His glance of amusement told her the answer and she added quickly: 'It's the best place to hear the whispers too, you know.'

'I think that was mentioned.' Another weed flew past Benny's ear. 'I used to think that in a controlled environment there wouldn't be any weeds,' he muttered. 'But that was before I discovered who has to do the controlling.'

Benny laughed. 'I'll leave you to it, Mister Crofton. I can see you're busy.'

He grunted. Then he straightened up and smiled, his face opening into a genuine expression of joy. 'Always a pleasure, Professor. It's nice to talk to someone who takes the trouble to appreciate my work.'

Benny smiled back. Evidently Mister Crofton had spoken recently to Ms Jones. There was a mutual lack of appreciation between them that went far deeper than the head groundsman's displeasure at being addressed shrilly as 'Crofton.'

He bent back to his work. Then paused, trowel in hand. 'Not looking for her, are you?'

They both knew he meant Ms Jones. 'No,' she said quickly, sharply. 'No,' she repeated more slowly and carefully. 'Not at all.' After a moment's consideration she added: 'Ha! The thought.'

He seemed satisfied at this. 'That's good. Thought you might have mislaid your thingummy again. Could lend you mine if you needed it.'

'Thanks,' she said. 'But I don't. Really. And anyway,' she added as she started across the lawn, 'it's biometrically coded. So nobody can use any one else's.'

All the same, she thought as she paused in the Summer-House to count the statues, she could have asked Mister Crofton to come and let her back into the Mansionhouse. Somewhere out there, she knew as she surveyed the expansive and impressive grounds, was a small round piece of pink plastic with her name on it and her DNA imprint encoded in it that would let her back inside the Mansionhouse. The prospect of searching the whole planet in the hope of finding where she had dropped it was daunting.

But it was nothing compared with the prospect of confessing to Ms Jones, Head of Administration, that she had lost it. Again.

It was difficult to tell where the scaffolding finished and the actual building began. The marble pillars, dark red veined with white, thrust upwards into the open air. Around them a network of metal poles and wooden boards allowed the workers to get at the upper level.

As he approached the peristyle frontage of the Grand Trianon, Vanderbilt could see the figures working on the stonework. The building seemed small by the standards of Braxiatel so far. Behind the row of pillars a small anti-grav crane was hoisting a long marble beam into position atop two of the pillars. The gardens that led up to the building were also incomplete. The turf was laid, and the beds cut out. But there was bare soil in the beds and the grass was roped off to protect the young lawn from careless feet.

It was only when he saw the cat meandering its carefree way between the pillars that he realised his mistake. The cat paused, moulding itself to the warm side of a sunlit pillar. As if to emphasise the point, one of the workers leant down and stroked the cat's tiny back. The cat allowed the attention for a moment, then darted out from under the hand and scurried through the gardens towards Vanderbilt.

His mistake had been to assume that the workers were human. He could see now as he grew closer, as he saw that the cat was not as small as it seemed, that the workers were far larger. The building was indeed immense, and so were the Killorans constructing it. It made sense, he thought as he bent to greet the cat. Her cat. Killorans were the best construction engineers and labourers money could hire. And Braxiatel certainly had money. One of them, he saw, was climbing down from the scaffolding and coming towards him as he lifted the cat and cradled it in his arms.

Vanderbilt stroked the cat's head gently, examining its front paws as he soothed it. 'There, there,' he murmured. 'Have we got a poorly foot? Now, let's have a look at that – does it hurt?' He massaged the paw gently, applying pressure as he listened to the cat's satisfied purr. 'Well, we'll have to do something about that, then, won't we?'

The cat struggled and gave a high-pitched squeal. Vanderbilt nodded as the sunlight was blotted out. 'I thought so. I saw you limping back there. A bit of a sprain perhaps. Actually, I think it's broken. We should bind it up.' He held the cat tightly as he looked up at the massive figure towering over him. 'Perhaps he caught it in something on the site?'

'Perhaps. I hadn't noticed.' The Killoran's voice was gruff and guttural. The grating snarls that punctuated the words were quite in keeping with its appearance – the rough accent more so. It was almost eight feet tall, big even for a Killoran. The hairy face wrinkled slightly as it extended a huge clawed paw to stroke the cat. Its touch was surprisingly gentle – for a creature that seemed to be a cross between an ape and an upright wolf, complete with dripping fangs. It was wearing blue overalls.

The cat settled slightly at the Killoran's touch, but Vanderbilt continued to hold it tight as it struggled to break free of his grasp.

'You shouldn't be here,' the Killoran remarked, turning its attention to Vanderbilt.

'Oh?'

It shook its shaggy head, snout curling back from the sharp teeth. 'Don't worry about it. We try to keep the construction areas clear so guests don't hurt themselves.'

'What about cats?'

'Wolsey?'

'If that's his name.'

'He goes where he likes.' The Killoran touched a small pink plastic disc attached to the cat's collar. 'Got his own tag.'

'So I see.' Vanderbilt waited a moment before he offered the Killoran his own disc. 'I guess you should see this.'

'That's all right, Dr Vanderbilt. But it's best to check.' The creature's snout edged upwards to reveal even more teeth. Perhaps it was a smile. 'My name's Wall,' he said. 'The name I use for humans, anyway. I'm in charge of all construction,' he added with obvious pride.

'A good choice of name then.' Vanderbilt knew that Killorans chose human-type names as their own were not easily pronounced by other races. Usually they opted for something grand and imposing, something imperial. Which seemed to Vanderbilt like a sensible idea. 'Is there somewhere I should take him?' he asked. 'To have his paw looked at?'

'Best take him up to the Mansionhouse. Ask for Benny, that is Professor Summerfield.' He seemed to shiver slightly as he added: 'Or Ms Jones.'

'Thank you.'

'That's all right,' Wall said as he turned back towards his construction site. 'Oi!' he bellowed across the nascent gardens. 'Julius – that's not where it goes.' He shook his enormous head in apparent disbelief. 'Excuse me,' he grunted as he lumbered off. 'Get Alex Thegrate to show you the plans before you go messing it all about, will you?' he shouted. 'I don't know, I despair. I really do.'

It was tempting to put the cat down. But he was afraid that he wouldn't see it again if he did, injured foot or not. He could hear the lock of the side door into the Mansionhouse click as he approached. Then the door didn't open. He tried it several times. And several times the door still didn't open. There was an intercom beside the door with a button below it. Vanderbilt was just coming to the conclusion that he would have to use it to ask to be let in, to get the cat seen to, when he heard the sound of running feet from behind him.

He recognised Professor Bernice Summerfield at once of course. The short black hair, informal dress – shorts, walking boots and khaki jacket – all matched the description he'd been given. The fact that she was more interested in the cat than she was in a strange man trying to enter a restricted area clinched it for him.

'Oh Wolsey,' she said, 'I was so worried. They told me you were hurt.' Her voice was cultured, clear. A happy, optimistic voice even through the concern. She scooped the cat from Vanderbilt's arms and held its face close to hers. Cheek

18

against cheek, they both seemed to purr.

Vanderbilt coughed politely. 'I was trying to get some help for him. He's hurt his paw. I'm afraid it may be broken. Is he your cat?' he added, though of course he knew.

'Wolsey,' she introduced the cat, waving its good front paw at him. 'And I'm Bernice – call me Benny.' She examined the paw, feeling delicately through the fur.

'I did think the door would open for him,' Vanderbilt said. 'I know my own disc won't let me in, but I thought…' He allowed his voice to tail off.

'There's a built-in mass detector. The system knows if he's being carried and so it checked your disc as well. He could get in on his own.' She held Wolsey in the crook of her arm as she reached over to press the button on the intercom. 'But you couldn't follow,' she added. 'He's got a cat flap.' She gave the button a good press, then said loudly: 'Professor Summerfield for Ms Jones. Urgently, please. Wolsey's hurt. And you are?'

It took him a moment to realise this last was addressed to him. 'Oh, er Vanderbilt. Dr Josiah Vanderbilt.' He gave a short sharp nod and clicked his heels politely.

'Here for the party?'

'Party? Oh, the millennium celebrations. Well, yes, of course.'

They shuffled their feet for several moments while they waited. They both flinched slightly at the tinny voice that erupted from the small speaker, set into the door frame.

'Is the little fellow all right?' The voice was thin and reedy, an artefact of the speaker Vanderbilt decided.

The door clicked and swung open.

'You'd better come in,' the voice said. 'Bring the poor thing straight down here, won't you.'

'Straight down here' turned out to be anything but straight. The route was a convolution of passageways and staircases that Vanderbilt committed to memory. It culminated in an imposing, heavy, dark wooden door with brass trimmings. A neatly-painted plaque at just above eye level stated: 'Administration'.

Vanderbilt noticed that Benny hesitated just slightly before knocking. Her eyes widened just a touch at the response from inside, and she took a deliberate breath before pushing open the door.

The room was large with a bare polished wooden floor. It was practically empty – no paintings, no statues, no ornaments. The only furniture was a large desk with a chair behind it. Evidently any visitors were expected to stand.

A large woman was behind the desk. Vanderbilt could see her over the top of the screen that jutted upwards at an angle from the desktop. Her grey hair was tied up in a bun on the top of her head, stretched back from her forehead so hard that her eyebrows seemed to have been pulled upwards with it. Her face was lined, broken by an angular nose that jutted forwards over thin bloodless lips.

She took off a pair of severe horn-rimmed spectacles and let them fall. They were attached to a chain round her neck and bounced off her enormous bosom as she rose to her feet. Which surprised Vanderbilt as he had thought she was already standing. She leaned forward so that she towered over Benny in front of the desk.

'Let's see the little chap,' the woman said, holding out her spade-like hands to take Wolsey. Vanderbilt stifled a smile. Her voice was exactly as it had sounded through the speaker – tinny, almost to the point of squeaky.

'It's his paw, Ms Jones,' Benny explained, pointing to it. 'I'm afraid it may be broken.' She glanced at Vanderbilt.

Ms Jones examined the injured paw carefully. 'Yes, yes, I see.' She put the cat down gently on her desk and pulled open a drawer. 'I'll just bind it up. He's in some pain, but with a dab of genetic binding ointment inside the bandage he'll soon be as good as new.' Her voice seemed to break, to drop a key as she added: 'Won't it, Wolsey.' She made some clicking noises with her tongue as she rummaged noisily through the contents of the drawer and eventually pulled out a roll of crêpe bandage.

'And where, may I ask, is your security disc, Bernice?' Ms Jones demanded as she carefully wound the bandage round Wolsey's paw. 'Hmm?'

'I'm sorry,' Benny mumbled, 'but I seem to have mislaid it.' Her eyes were shining and Vanderbilt thought she was trying not to smile. 'I was so concerned about Wolsey, I just must have dropped it. I guess.'

Vanderbilt was not taken in for a second. Nor, he thought, was Wolsey who was now licking dubiously at the knot of bandage round his paw.

But Ms Jones immediately softened. 'Of course. The little fellow must come first, mustn't he. Should be all right now though. All sorted out, aren't we, hmmm?' She lifted Wolsey up and passed him back to Benny. He rolled on his back in her arms and purred gently, sparing a moment to shoot a dignified look of disdain at Vanderbilt.

'I hope you haven't come to tell me that you've lost your security pass?' Ms Jones demanded, turning her severe attention to Vanderbilt.

He held up his hands to stay her wrath. 'Indeed not. I was merely helping minister to the injured.' He held out his hand, his real hand. 'Dr Josiah Vanderbilt.'

She ignored the gesture. 'Hmm,' she said and returned to rummaging in the drawer of the desk. She pulled out a pink plastic disc and slapped it into Benny's waiting hand. 'Good,' Ms Jones said to Vanderbilt. 'Because while I have found it prudent to keep a supply of spare discs for Professor Summerfield, I have very few spares suitable for other guests.'

'Thank you so much,' Benny said as she pocketed the disc. 'He'll be fine now.'

'I expect so,' Ms Jones replied, as if Benny had been asking for an opinion rather than expressing one. 'How did he get hurt?'

'I found him limping by one of the construction sites,' Vanderbilt explained. 'He seemed in some pain.'

'The anaesthetic in the bandage should sort that out.' Ms Jones was jabbing at a keypad in front of her screen. 'I should have known that Wall would be at the bottom of this. Him or Crofton.'

'Mister Crofton,' Benny murmured. But she was ignored.

'I'll call him up and give him a piece of my mind.'

'Please don't,' Benny said. 'I'm sure it wasn't Adrian's fault.'

Ms Jones seemed to relent and waved a hand at the screen dismissively. 'I should you know,' she said, but her tone was lighter now. 'I don't know what you'd all do without me here to look after things.' She shook her head. 'I should tell that so-called Construction Manager what his name really means. That will teach him.'

'Don't you dare,' Benny snapped back. Her insistence surprised Vanderbilt. 'I told you that in confidence. He'd be devastated if he found out. He thinks that Adrian Wall was a great ancient Roman emperor who was responsible for defending England against the Scots. And I don't want him to learn any different.'

'Hmmm,' Ms Jones said. She seemed subdued by Benny's outburst. 'All right then.' She took a great bosom-heaving breath that jangled her spectacles. 'Now then, be off with you. Both of you. I have a hundred and one impossible things to do before this evening's festivities.' She shook her head. 'What Mr Braxiatel would do without me to sort things out, I really have no idea. Run along.' She made shooing gestures with her enormous hands as she settled back down into her chair.

They ran along. Vanderbilt followed Benny back through the maze of corridors and stairs towards the door. The last thing he wanted was to be evicted from the Mansionhouse now he had got this far. This close.

'Will he be all right now?' His voice was laced with concern.

'Yeah. Fine.' Benny paused and turned Wolsey so that Vanderbilt could see him. The cat's eyes narrowed to slits as it returned his stare.

'I should like to be sure,' he said slowly. 'I don't want to think the poor thing might still be in some pain.'

'Another ten minutes and I can take the bandage off. In a day he'll be right as rain.' She started down the corridor again. The eyes of the portraits that hung on the panelled walls watched Vanderbilt as he followed. 'He'll be fine. Really.'

She stopped abruptly half way along the corridor. 'I'm sorry,' she said as she turned back to him again. 'I'm forgetting my manners.' She smiled. 'My room's just along there. Why don't you come and have a glass of wine and you can watch when I remove Wolsey's bandage?'

'I don't want to be any trouble,' Vanderbilt said hesitantly. 'I shouldn't really be here, you know.'

'Oh nonsense,' she snorted. 'We have you to thank for finding him. He might have been wandering about out there for ever with an broken foot if you hadn't found him.'

Vanderbilt shrugged. 'If I wouldn't be in your way. I should like to check he really is okay.' He kept his expression neutral, blank. But inside he was smiling.

The living area of the ground floor of the Mansionhouse was far more spacious and impressive than the back corridors and stairways that Vanderbilt had so far seen. As Benny led him to her room, the ceilings seemed to become higher, the passages lighter and wider. The dull portraits on the walls were superseded by bright landscapes. In every alcove stood a statue or a piece of antique furniture.

After what seemed an age, they arrived in a large lobby area. The floor was dark marble with a circular design inlaid in the centre. There were several doors off the lobby. Benny went to one of them and opened it. She went in without looking to see if Vanderbilt was following.

He supposed the room was a study. There was a large desk on the far side of the room, facing a huge bay window that took up most of the wall. Through the window he could see the main lawn as it sloped away from the Mansionhouse. The impression he got of the room was the trappings of comfort. The walls were lined with red silk and hung with portraits framed with heavy gilt. An ornate Harastian wall mirror was hanging on one side of the desk, with with looked like the original of Constable's 'The Hay Wain'. The opposite wall was dominated by a huge marble fireplace. A deep rug ran almost to the sides of the room, the onyx floor visible as a margin round the edge. High above him as he walked slowly in and looked round, was a huge, gilt chandelier.

Benny was disappearing through an inner door. He caught a glimpse of a four-poster bed in the room beyond and a muddled impression of what looked like heaps of clothing on the floor.

'Help yourself to a glass,' Benny's voice floated back to him. 'On the desk. I'm just going to bathe his paw.'

In amongst the assortment of notebooks, pencils and reference volumes on the desk were a couple of bottles of wine. Both were open, both were half empty. Several glasses jutted upwards from the sea of papers, and Vanderbilt pulled one free with his left hand. He held it up to the light in an attempt to see if it had been used. It was difficult to tell.

But the wine was not his main concern. He glanced again at the open door to the bedroom, and satisfied that there was no sign of Benny, he carefully opened the top drawer of the desk.

By the time Benny returned, rubbing her knuckles gently across the top of Wolsey's head, Vanderbilt was sitting on a chaise longue sipping a glass of red wine. He got quickly to his feet. 'How is he?'

'He's fine. Thank you.' She set Wolsey down on the rug, stroking his back for a moment before he ran off, still limping, back towards the bedroom. She watched him go.

'Seems to have unsettled him a bit,' Vanderbilt said. 'I'm not surprised, poor thing.'

Benny poured herself some of the wine. 'Josiah, didn't you

say?' she asked.

'What? Oh, yes. Josiah Vanderbilt.' He gave a short bow. 'At your service.'

'Really?' She smiled and looked him up and down. 'Enjoy your wine,' she said.

Instead he set the half-full glass down on the edge of the desk. 'I should be going, really. I haven't even unpacked yet.'

'Oh.' She almost sounded disappointed.

He was tempted to stay and finish the wine, but speed was important. 'Will you excuse me?'

'Of course.'

He turned to the door. At the same moment as there was a loud knock. His hand ducked instinctively inside his jacket, but closed on nothing.

'It's open,' Benny called, oblivious.

He stood rigid as the door opened. Standing there was a tall man with short dark hair. He was not exactly thin, but his features were angular. He was wearing a light grey suit that was somehow at once smart and casual. When he spoke his voice was deep and smooth and clear. 'I hope I'm not intruding, Benny.'

'Of course not.'

'I was just leaving. There's no problem,' Vanderbilt said. He was unsettled by the way the man's eyes were forever moving, darting to and fro, absorbing every detail of him. Vanderbilt smiled thinly as the man stood aside and let him though the door.

He knew who the man was, of course. And Irving Braxiatel was one of the last people he wanted to see right now.

Benny sighed as she watched him go. 'I think you scared him off,' she told Braxiatel.

'That wasn't my intention, I assure you.'

'Never mind. Drink?'

'Not for me.' He settled himself down on the chaise longue that the tall blond man had vacated. 'I got some garbled message from Ms Jones about Wolsey.'

Benny smiled. 'He's fine. Caught his foot on something in the grounds. Josiah found him. He was quite concerned.' She reached for the bottle and held it up for Braxiatel to see.

He shook his head. 'Josiah?' Braxiatel frowned.

'Yes. He's a bit shy I think. But a sweetie really.' She put the bottle down again. 'Sure you won't?'

'Quite sure.' His voice was distant, thoughtful. 'The only Josiah I can think of is old Vanderbilt.'

Benny topped up her glass. 'That's right. Dr Josiah Vanderbilt. I don't know what he's a doctor of, mind you. He didn't say.'

'Organic crystallography, amongst other things.' He still seemed thoughtful, absorbed.

'Well there you go then.' Benny sipped at the wine. It was warm and viscous. 'You know him?'

'Oh yes. I know Dr Josiah Vanderbilt.'

She sensed there was more. 'And?'

'And that wasn't him.'

Benny considered this, forcing the wine through her teeth and letting the flavour soak into the depths of her mouth. 'Oh,' she said at last. 'Sure?'

'I only invited Vanderbilt as a courtesy really,' Braxiatel told her. He got to his feet and went over to the desk.

'You know about courtesy then,' Benny quipped.

He took it in the spirit it was intended. 'I know about many things,' he said. 'For example, I know never to raise my hands to a lady.'

'And why's that?' she asked.

He told her. And they both laughed. 'Poor old Vanderbilt is in his eighties,' Braxiatel said. 'He doesn't get out much these days.'

'He probably doesn't raise anything to a lady,' Benny said.

Braxiatel did not seem to hear her. He pulled a silk handkerchief from his top pocket and waved it at the half-full wine glass on the edge of the desk. 'This his?'

Benny nodded. 'Could be his son maybe?' Braxiatel's look was sufficient for her to revise her opinion. 'Grandson?'

'I don't think so.' Braxiatel was lifting the glass up and examining it carefully, holding it delicately in the handkerchief. 'Talcum powder,' he said with a note of decision.

'I'm sorry?'

'Do you have some? And one of those fluffy puffy pink things women use to dab it about with, whatever they're called.'

'They're called fluffy puffy things,' Benny told him. 'And mine is yellow.'

When he had finished, they both stood looking up at the glass as Braxiatel twisted it round. The outside of the bowl was frosted with a thin layer of fine white talcum. The light from the chandelier was diffused through it, misty.

'I saw him holding it,' Benny said. 'He was sitting facing this way, so it was in his left hand.'

Braxiatel sighed. He lowered the glass and wiped the talcum from one side. 'So either he has no fingerprints...' He inspected the results of his polishing, then downed the wine in a gulp.

'Or?' Benny prompted.

'Or he doesn't sweat.'

'I don't sweat,' Benny said brightly. She laughed at his confused expression. 'Horses sweat,' she explained. 'Men perspire.' She grinned at him. 'I just glow.'

Braxiatel clicked his tongue. 'And I'd put that down to the wine,' he said.

It clicked off at the wrist. The whole of his left hand pulled away from the forearm. It was attached by a twisted line of wires that now stretched out across the low coffee table. He flexed his fingers. It always amused him to see them move on their own.

With his other hand – his real hand – he reached inside the stump of the wrist and pulled out an FTL accelerator card. It had built in encryption as well as the faster than light circuits, and it snapped into the standard socket on the local communications system. There was a handset by the bed.

On the whole, the man who was not Vanderbilt thought as he clicked his hand back into place, he rather liked it here. He had a small thatched cottage on the outskirts of the Hamlet. Suitably isolated and quiet, just what he would have chosen himself. The ceilings were a little low and he would have liked more space, but it would do. He had stayed in worse places. It was clean and tidy and he wasn't sharing it with the rats and the dead.

'Keep it brief, this could be traced.' Kendrick's voice was a harsh grating from the speaker.

Vanderbilt doubted he was right, but he didn't argue. Not with Kendrick. 'Everything's on schedule,' he reported. 'No problems.'

'You have it? You got the –'

'Yes, I got it. It's digitised and uploading now so you should be able to get your expert to insert it into the material and send it on to me in plenty of time.'

'Excellent. You've done well.'

'Thank you, sir.' He tried not to sound surprised. It wasn't often one got praise from Marshal Raul Kendrick. 'Let's hope the rest of the operation goes as well.'

'Yes, let's hope so.'

Vanderbilt's thin smile faded. Kendrick's sentiment was innocent enough. But his tone had made it sound like a threat.

'Match found,' the inhuman female voice intoned without emotion.

Grudgingly, Benny had cleared enough of her desk for Braxiatel to get at her computer. He had used his personal security clearance to pull up footage from the surveillance cameras at the side door and found the point where Vanderbilt – whoever he really was – and Benny had waited with Wolsey.

A pattern recognition and matching program that Braxiatel admitted he just happened to have written when he was bored one afternoon was now trying to identify the freeze-framed face of Vanderbilt.

'So who is he?' Benny asked.

'Voice print not authorised,' the female voice told her coldly.

'So who is he?' Braxiatel asked.

'Match found in secure Fifth Axis Central Records System.'

Benny laughed. 'Not that secure then.'

Braxiatel waved her to silence as the voice continued.

'Subject identified as Kolonel Daglan Straklant, Fifth Axis Security Elite.'

Benny and Braxiatel looked at each other for a while without speaking. Then Benny said: 'I take it that's not good.'

'On the whole, no. Not good.'

'Oops?' she suggested.

Braxiatel nodded. He turned back to examine the frozen face on the screen. 'Oops,' he agreed.

2
Opening Night

The festivities were held in the main rooms of the ground floor of the Mansionhouse with guests spilling out into the gardens behind. There was sufficient food, more than enough drink, and the promise of spectacular fireworks. Braxiatel had been telling anyone he spoke to, in confidence, that he was slightly worried that he might have gone overboard on the fireworks and there was a real possibility that setting them off might knock the small planetoid off its orbit. It had the desired effect – everyone was awaiting the display with a mixture of awe and trepidation.

'I don't see him,' Benny told Braxiatel as they met beside a pyramid of champagne glasses. She had toyed with the idea of coming along in her jeans and a t-shirt. But after due consideration she had settled for a bright blue ballgown.

'Pity,' Braxiatel said, handing Benny a flute of champagne. 'I'd like to ask him what he's up to.'

She wrinkled her nose as she sipped at the bubbly liquid. 'I'd have thought that, given the occasion, you'd have gone for those champagne glasses that are modelled on the shape of Marie Antoinette's breasts,' she said.

Braxiatel smiled and chinked his glass against Benny's. 'A nice sentiment,' he said. 'But sadly they're about as good at keeping a decent head in place as she was. Cheers.'

'Cheers.'

Braxiatel made a point of circulating and greeting everyone like long-lost friends. Which, Benny thought, most of them probably were. For her own part, she made a point of keeping out of most people's way. She was enjoying the champagne and the nibbles and the atmosphere. The occasion. The setting, the evening, the background music and the evident and open enjoyment of everyone were all things to be savoured. Later, yes, later she would make conversation and be witty and frothy and personable.

Further down the enormous ballroom she could see Adrian Wall and a group of his Killoran colleagues standing together. They were laughing loudly and enthusiastically, holding what looked like pints of ale though Benny had no idea where they'd got them. Smuggled in, perhaps. They all looked like they had been forcibly jammed into their suits, probably by means of creative application of some of their own construction equipment.

Benny's suspicion about the unofficial nature of the ale was confirmed as Ms Jones marched forward across the room in their direction. Her loose dress flapped round her like a torn sail in a tempest and her high heels ricocheted off the polished floor. Her glasses hung incongruously over her exposed cleavage. The crowd parted for her, unbidden. The glasses of ale disappeared inside jackets and behind backs. One Killoran handed his glass to a nearby guest who stared at the pint mug in some disbelief.

There were expressions of genuine fear on the faces of some of the Killorans as Ms Jones approached them. They turned to sighs of relief as she swept past, and the ale reappeared from its inadequate concealment. Ms Jones marched on, oblivious.

It was only as she grew closer that Benny began to suspect that she might herself be the intended target of whatever the Head of Administration was about to unleash.

'I thought so,' Ms Jones proclaimed shrilly. She shook her head in annoyance so that her glasses jangled.

'Something wrong?' Benny asked, hoping she sounded sympathetic and helpful.

'Honestly.' She waved a hand at the table beside Benny. 'I ask you. I mean, you can see, can't you?'

'I can?' Benny looked.

There were several plates of finger food on the table. Ms Jones pointed at one. 'We're nearly out of these cheesey-pineapple things on sticks. They really must make a better job of keeping these platters stocked.' She gave a mighty 'harumph' and continued on her way, heading for the door. Her voice floated back towards Benny as she made her exit. 'What he'd do without me here to sort things out I really cannot imagine…'

Eventually and inevitably Benny got caught up in conversation. She had moved outside. The night was clear and still and as it approached midnight, people drifted out into the grounds. She was surprised to see Mister Crofton awkwardly holding a glass of champagne and waved to him across several low hedges. He smiled and waved back.

'Excuse me, but you look like you know your way around.' She turned to see a diffident looking man, short and stocky and sweating. His shirt needed to be tucked in and his lank hair had flopped forward so that it almost covered one eye. He flicked it aside with a quick nervous gesture.

'Oh?' Benny said in what she hoped was not a tone that committed her to anything.

'Only I was wondering if…' He paused, swallowed, looked around and lowered his voice to a husky whisper. '…If you knew where the toilets are?'

'Not the best chat-up line I've ever heard,' Benny told him. 'But it does win points for originality,' she conceded. 'I'm Benny, by the way. And yes I do know where the toilets are, thank you.'

He waited for a moment, then seemed to realise that she wasn't going to say any more. 'Oh, er, sorry. Dale Pettit. I'm an authority on genetics,' he added, as if he hoped this would help.

'I'm pleased to meet you,' Benny replied. She toyed briefly with the idea of seeing how long she could keep him standing there before he got desperate and ran off. But his damp face was already beginning to contort and he was moving his ample weight from one foot to the other. So she settled for telling him that she reckoned geneticists really should be doing something about fixing the whole toilet business for the convenience, if that was the best word, of future generations, then directing him through the ballroom to the nearest men's room. 'And if there's a queue, try at the top of the main staircase, just outside the Archaeology Department,' she added. 'That's signposted – the Archaeology Department, not the staircase.'

'Thank you,' he said hurriedly.

He was out of sight before the 'You're welcome' had reached Benny's front teeth. It was ten minutes later that Braxiatel found her.

He was hopelessly lost. After what seemed a promising start, his attempted exploration of the Mansionhouse, centrepiece of the Braxiatel Collection, had gone rather wrong. But despite being in a corridor he could not remember ever seeing before, approaching a door he had never opened, the distant sounds of the celebrations downstairs and outside gave him confidence that he could find his way back if and when he needed to.

Until he saw the light.

There was a gap at the bottom of the door where it did not quite meet the polished wooden floor. And visible through that gap, playing back and forth just for an instant, was a light. A flashlight. Someone was inside the room. Someone who did not wish to turn on the main lights.

His curiosity piqued, he eased the door open slowly and quietly.

But not quietly enough.

The room was massive, its edges lost in shadows. Isolated by the torchlight perhaps ten yards away, was a man. He was shining the flashlight at a shelf. He was frozen in the light, caught in the midst of sliding something on to, or off, the shelf. His face was turned towards the door.

'You idiot,' a voice hissed across the darkness, echoing in the shadows. 'You've triggered the alarm.' The man placed the flashlight on the shelf, wedging it between books so that it faced back at the door. Dazzling bright.

Then the man was running towards him, holding whatever he had taken from the shelf in one hand. And in the other...

34

'And you've seen me,' the harsh whisper continued.

'Have you seen Broderick?' Braxiatel asked. He was frowning.

'Might have done.'

He breathed out heavily with relief. 'Oh good. He's supposed to be setting off the fireworks, but I haven't seen him. There's less than twenty minutes to go.'

'Irving,' Benny said heavily, 'I wasn't being funny. I wouldn't know Broderick Naismith if I did see him. We've never met.'

'Really?' He seemed surprised. 'Well, when I find him I'll make sure I introduce you.'

'Thanks. You know for a Chief Publicity Relations Officer, or whatever he's supposed to be, he doesn't seem very keen to promote himself to the rest of us.'

'Now that's hardly fair,' Braxiatel said. 'He's a busy man. Not only does he handle all the publicity and media relations, but he also –' He broke off as he saw that Benny's attention was not entirely focused on his words.

'You're flashing,' she told him. 'Did you know?'

'I beg your pardon?' Braxiatel blinked and looked down.

'No, no. Your pen. The top of it is flashing.' Benny plucked it from his top pocket and handed it to him. The end of the pen was flashing bright red. 'I've studied *Thunderbirds*,' she said, 'so I know it's important. Whatever it is.'

His face was serious as he took the pen. She could see that there was a tiny screen set into the side of the pen and struggled to make out what was on it.

'It used to be a teapot, didn't it?' Braxiatel said as he clicked the pen and the flashing stopped.

'You used to keep a teapot in your pocket?' The image was bizarre but she could quite believe it.

'I meant in *Thunderbirds*,' he told her. 'Come on.'

'Where to?'

'The Archaeology Department. That was an intruder alarm.'

They managed not to seem as if they were hurrying unduly

as they eased their way through the crowds and out of the back of the ballroom. Braxiatel led the way, taking the stairs two at a time. Benny had to gather her dress and hoist it up over her calves to have any hope of following.

'All right for those with long legs,' she grumbled breathlessly as she followed. She knew Braxiatel well enough to know he wouldn't wait for her. And he didn't.

She caught up with him at the entrance to the Archaeology Department. He paused just inside the door to activate the main lights. In a moment the huge concourse was bathed in soft yellow light. Benny gasped.

The room was enormous – at least a hundred metres long and ten metres wide. It was loosely modelled on the Hall of Battles at Versailles. The polished floor seemed to go on forever beneath a ceiling which curved up to a glass roof. During the day, the sunlight shone in bands between the leading and soaked one side of the concourse in yellow. But now everywhere was washed with the even amber glow of the artificial lighting, the shadows banished. The sides of the concourse were lined from floor to ceiling with shelves. Each shelf, Benny knew, was meticulously bar-coded, struggling to hold the weight of the documents, discs, optical spheres and other storage media jammed on to it.

At intervals across the width of the room were pillared partitions with wooden desks against them. Here those researchers lucky enough to be granted access to the Collection would soon be able to work in silence, lost deep in piles of paper and storage media or engrossed in the graphics and read-outs which played across the desktop terminals. Benny had tested the facilities exhaustively.

She had also tried out the holographic simulation suites off the main concourse, as well as secondary storage areas, 'personal facilities' and a small room where the Archivist on duty could make tea.

Whenever she came into the Archaeology Department she was overawed by the immensity and splendour of it. But now she gasped in surprise rather than in awe.

About fifteen feet from where she stood, two men were fighting. She could see that one of them was Vanderbilt – or rather Straklant. The other man had his back to her, and a knife at Vanderbilt's throat.

Vanderbilt saw Benny at the same time as she saw him. Despite the situation, he smiled. The combination of this and the lights seemed to break his attacker's concentration and he turned slightly, his attention disturbed.

Benny gasped again as she saw that it was Dale Pettit. 'Toilet man,' she murmured.

But her quiet words were obscured by Vanderbilt's shout as he suddenly broke Pettit's hold and knocked the knife away. With his other hand, his left hand, he smashed Pettit to the floor with a sudden and violent blow to the head.

For a moment Benny's view was obscured by Braxiatel as he ran forwards. When he moved aside, Benny could see Pettit lying on the floor. He was on his back, his head twisted to the side. His eyes were staring wide and empty at Benny, and a viscous trickle of red eased round his head and pooled on the polished wood of the floor.

Then the room exploded.

The sound was incredible, a blast of noise that threatened to rupture the eardrums. The whole of the glassed ceiling was crazed with stabs of bright light. The sky was on fire, alive with multicoloured sparks and flame.

Braxiatel bent to recover the knife. He wasted no more than a few seconds checking on Pettit, then turned his attention to Vanderbilt and Benny.

'Happy new year,' he said grimly as another Skutloid's Glitter Glory exploded in the festive night sky.

'You say he was trying to take this?' Braxiatel held up the leather case.

Vanderbilt nodded. 'I didn't mean to kill him,' he said. He sounded embarrassed more than contrite. 'I have an artificial hand. It's rather heavier than it looks. I tend to forget my own strength.'

'No fingerprints,' Benny said quietly to Braxiatel.

He nodded. 'Just tell us what happened,' he said to Vanderbilt. 'What were you doing here?' He paused before adding: 'Dr Vanderbilt.'

He did not seem to notice Braxiatel's ironic tone. 'I confess I was a bit lost. Thought I'd have a look round while everyone was at the party.' Vanderbilt gave a half-smile and shrugged. 'I know I should have asked, really. But anyway, I saw a light. He was taking that off a shelf when I opened the door.'

'Good job you did,' Benny said. 'That's what set off the alarm. Any idea how Pettit bypassed it?' she asked Braxiatel.

'None. Yet.'

'Anyway,' Vanderbilt went on, 'I challenged the man, and he went for me.' He smiled, almost apologetically. 'With a knife.'

'A somewhat extreme reaction,' Braxiatel said slowly.

'I'll say,' Vanderbilt agreed.

'He means,' Benny explained, 'considering the guy could just have asked to see the document. Whatever it is,' she added, shooting a look at Braxiatel.

Her question was not lost on him. 'I'll check on that in a moment. It's a holosphere, but I'll need to cross reference the index code to find out exactly what it is. That can wait.'

'Oh?'

'Yes. I'll put it in my study. It'll be safe there. But now I think we should get back to the celebrations, don't you?'

'Worried about being a party pooper?' Benny asked. 'Or an inattentive host?'

Braxiatel headed towards the door. 'I'm worried people may start to talk,' he said. 'I'd rather nobody knew there was anything wrong here.'

'And after the celebrations are over?' Vanderbilt asked. 'What then?'

'Then I suggest you both get some sleep. I'd like us all to meet up in the morning to go over this again. By then I should know something about the holosphere and what it contains. And about this Dale Pettit.' He paused in the doorway, staring back at the supine body illuminated by the maelstrom of light from outside.

'Don't you need sleep?' Vanderbilt asked, raising an eyebrow.

'No,' Benny told him. 'No, he doesn't.'

Braxiatel led them to the door, locking it once they were outside. 'If we hurry, we might just catch the end of the fireworks. I'll see you in my study first thing,' Braxiatel said. They started down the main staircase.

Benny shook her head. 'Second thing. Coffee is the first thing. Always.' She gave a short laugh. 'You know,' she told Braxiatel, 'you're going to have to stop holding parties. Someone always sees it as an excuse to cause trouble. Remember the Delvians at that black tie bash the other week?'

Braxiatel smiled. 'But surely,' he said, 'that's half the fun of it.' He held Benny's arm gently as they walked, holding her back to let Vanderbilt get a few stairs ahead. 'One thought,' Braxiatel murmured.

'Yes?'

'There's a dead body back there in the Archaeology Department. A bit of a mess.'

She nodded. 'I did notice actually,' she whispered back.

'Ms Jones will need to arrange to have it, er, tidied.'

'Good idea.'

She felt his grip tighten slightly and turned in time to see him swallow. He seemed to have gone rather pale. 'I'm, er, going to be rather busy,' he mumbled. 'Checking up on things. Perhaps you could have a word with her.'

Benny widened her eyes, as if not getting his gist.

'For me,' he said. Then, with a hint of desperation in his tone: 'Please?'

It was almost three in the morning when Benny tumbled into her room. She wasn't entirely sure that the ceiling ought to be wobbling about quite as much as it seemed to be, and paused to stare at it for a minute in the hope that it might settle down a bit.

When it didn't, she kicked off her shoes, took a step forwards, and fell over the parcel that was on the floor in front of her. She sat looking at it for a while, trying to focus on the patterned wrapping paper. Eventually, she decided it must be meant to look fuzzy like that, and picked it up. Sitting cross-legged on the floor, her ballgown hitched up over her knees, she turned the parcel over looking for some clue as to where it had come from.

'My birthday,' she said firmly and with only a slight effort, 'is June the twenty-first.' She nodded, convinced that was right. 'And today is January the first. Which makes this,' she decided, 'a new year's present.'

Happy that this must be the case, she ripped the paper off.

Inside was a wooden box. It was polished and attractive, about the size of a shoe box. Benny undid the clip and lifted the lid, peering in. Why did someone think she needed a box?

It almost took her head off. She jerked back just in time, the room swimming round her with the sudden movement. A plain white sphere, slightly larger than Benny's clenched fist, had floated out of the box and was now bobbing gently in front of her. Benny looked at the sphere. Benny looked into the box, and saw that it was lined with felt, a round hole scooped out where the sphere had been lying. Benny looked back at the sphere. And it spoke.

'Greetings, Professor Bernice Summerfield.' Its voice was slightly nasal, its tone implied that this was the sphere's room and Benny was the uninvited and unwanted guest.

'Hi, Joseph,' she said weakly. The ceiling was doing its wobble thing again.

'That is indeed the nomenclature that Mr Braxiatel imbued me with at initial program load.'

'Figures,' Benny said. 'I wonder which he needs to work on first – his tact or his sense of humour.'

'Professor?'

'Call me Benny.' She struggled to her feet. 'You always did.'

'I am aware,' the sphere told her as it bobbed dangerously close to her head, 'that you previously had a personal intelligent organisational assistant with identical nomenclature and comparable facilities.'

'I think there was a bit more to him than that,' Benny said. 'Or less, depending on how you look at it.'

But the sphere, Joseph, wasn't listening. 'I am imbued with the ability to organise your diary and schedule, to link into the Braxiatel Collection mainframes and access administrative and scheduling data on your behalf, cross-check diaries and appointment books, and perform online calendar management tasks.'

'Mmm. Very impressive.' Benny risked cocking her head to one side. She could feel her brain sloshing about in the champagne as she moved, but reckoned the effect was worth the discomfort. 'Can you do anything useful?' she asked. 'At all?'

'Er,' Joseph squeaked. 'Well...'

Benny smiled. It had been worth it.

'I can ensure that your personal chronometer is synched with the temporal satellite signalling system on any civilised world.'

She nodded slowly. 'You mean, you can set my watch to the right time? Great. Terrific. Tell you what,' she said, 'let's do that tomorrow.'

'Yes, Professor,' Joseph said dubiously.

She bent down and carefully lifted the wooden box, holding it open. 'Right now it's time for bed.'

Joseph dipped and spun enthusiastically. 'While you sleep, Professor, I am tasked to tidy and dust your residential area.'

'No you're not,' she told him, grabbing for the wooden box. 'Get inside.'

'Inside... the box?' It almost sounded as if Joseph had gulped.

Benny jiggled the box in what she hoped was a suitably threatening manner. 'In,' she said forcefully.

'I am concerned,' Joseph squeaked as he lowered himself gently on to the felt lining, that you are not making the fullest and best use of my – '

But whatever Benny was not making the fullest and best use of became an indecipherable squawk as she closed the lid and snapped the catch shut. Then she breathed a sigh of relief and put the box down on top of a lot of other stuff on her desk. She looked at it for a moment, then slumped into the chair behind the desk and put her head in her hands.

It was a kind thought, she decided. Kind of Braxiatel to give her a present. Kind of him to make it something useful. Kind of him to restore something of her past, something to make her feel at home. Something she had thought was lost forever. Something she had missed.

'Oh Jason, Jason,' she sobbed into her hands. 'I miss you so much.'

She didn't know or care how long she wept. She didn't know or care if Joseph could hear her from inside his box – if he was even 'awake', whatever that meant to him. But eventually she wiped her eyes on the back of her hand. She leaned down and pulled open one of the desk drawers. Inside was a heap of papers and a stack of exercise books.

Benny spent a few minutes rummaging in the drawer, getting gradually more worried and frantic. She took out each of the notebooks in turn and shook it to see what fell out. Nothing.

She checked the other drawers. Still nothing. But somewhere, in a drawer or amongst the heaps of debris on the top of the desk, she knew there was a photograph. Old fashioned and low-tech, sentimental and silly. But it was her favourite picture of Jason. A memory that right now she could do with. And like so much of her life, it seemed to have slipped out of reach.

Her head slumped forward on the desk. She pushed her arms out to make room and heard the things falling as they toppled over the edge. She didn't care. Benny sat there till she fell asleep, lost in her memories, her love, and her tears.

* * *

They were in Braxiatel's study on the first floor of the Manionhouse. Benny had arrived before Vanderbilt, and thanked Braxiatel for his gift.

'I thought it might help you feel at home,' he told her. And she could tell that he meant it.

'Thanks,' she said. 'Though I don't promise to play with him every day.'

At that moment there was a knock at the door. Without any apparent help from anyone, the door swung slowly open.

Benny was pleased to see that Vanderbilt seemed impressed when he entered. The walls of Braxiatel's study were inlaid marble, the floor flagged with stone. The ceiling was covered with a perfect replica of *The Supremacy of Venus* – the goddess sitting amongst the clouds surrounded by cherubs and maidens. In the centre of the large room stood a mahogany writing desk. Braxiatel was sitting in a simple office chair behind it. He was leaning forwards, his hands resting on the blotter in the centre of the desk. Beside them lay a heavy silver fountain pen. At the front of the desk was a small plaque which read: 'Custodian of the Library of St John the Beheaded.'

Along each wall were alcoves. In several stood statues of Levithian Graffs in full ceremonial armour. Others were empty, the walls blank. Benny knew that they were awaiting paintings of parts of the grounds that had yet to be created. Once painted, these would be to make up for the lack of windows. The room was deep within the Mansionhouse – not overlooked.

Against one wall was a plush leather sofa, where Benny was now sitting. A door beside the sofa led into Braxiatel's living quarters. Vanderbilt sat uneasily on an upright chair in front of the desk where Braxiatel was presiding. Like a schoolboy in front of his headmaster, Benny thought.

'Tea?' Braxiatel asked.

'Ms Jones had the body removed,' Benny said once they all

43

had a cup, by way of making conversation.

Braxiatel nodded. 'She sent me a DNA profile to help trace who Dale Pettit really was.'

Benny and Vanderbilt both leaned forward, teacups held firmly in front of them.

'And?' Benny said.

'Who was he?' Vanderbilt asked.

'He was Dale Pettit, I'm afraid.' Braxiatel smiled at their expressions. 'Yes, I was a bit disappointed too. He really was who he claimed to be. A research graduate invited as representative of the New Adventura Institute of Cross-Licensing and Print Merchandise.' He sipped at his tea. 'I don't know why they bothered, frankly.'

'Maybe because of what he hoped to steal?' Benny suggested.

'Maybe.' Braxiatel tapped his fingers on the leather case that lay on the blotter in front of him. 'But this isn't restricted. It doesn't even seem to have been catalogued, actually. Which is something of an oversight. It is of some academic interest, however.' He sighed and sat back in his chair. 'If only everyone were simply what they seemed to be, life would be so much more…' He waved a hand as if hoping to conjure the word out of the surrounding air.

'Uninteresting?' Benny volunteered.

Vanderbilt coughed and moved uneasily on his chair. 'Before we go on,' he said, 'I, er, I think I should just clarify one thing.' He looked from Braxiatel to Benny.

'Oh?' Benny said, all innocence and naivety.

'Yes… Dr Vanderbilt?' Braxiatel asked.

'Yes, well, that's it, really,' Vanderbilt said. He licked his lips and looked at his feet. His voice was stronger, more determined, as he looked up again and said: 'I'm not actually Josiah Vanderbilt.'

'Well,' Benny said levelly. 'There's a thing.'

Braxiatel leaned forwards. 'I'm grateful for your honesty, Kolonel Straklant,' he said. 'Please do explain.'

'Ah.' The man who had claimed to be Vanderbilt looked

even more uncomfortable now. He brushed back his immaculately tidy fair hair with his hand. 'So you know.'

'We'd still like an explanation,' Benny told him. 'Why would a Kolonel in the Fifth Axis Security Elite want to pretend to be a doctor of organic whatever-it-is? Come to that,' she said to Braxiatel, 'what the hell is the Fifth Axis when it's at home?'

'It's a particularly ambitious and totalitarian regime that should have stayed at home,' Braxiatel said, his good-natured smile made heavy by his tone. 'Wouldn't you agree, Kolonel?'

'I'd rather not get into a discussion of politics, if you don't mind,' Straklant said. 'Other than to point out that no representative of the Fifth Axis was invited to your impressive opening event, so we had to resort to a small deception in order to gain admission.'

'Is that reasonable?' Benny asked.

'That depends on what you mean by reasonable,' Braxiatel said. His eyes were levelled at Straklant. 'An ambitious territorial power that is advancing through neutral space without permission, subjugating anyone and anything that gets in its way can probably be forgiven a small deception, as you call it. Though I confess I am surprised.'

'Oh?' Straklant said.

Braxiatel drained his tea and returned the cup to the saucer. 'You're looting art and archaeology treasures from across the so-called Assimilated Territories without any regard for their provenance, value, historical interest or ownership. I'm surprised you couldn't just wait till your armies reach us and then take whatever you want.' He poured himself more tea. 'Or am I missing something?' he asked over-politely.

'With due respect, sir,' Straklant said, with an obvious effort to keep his tone and manner polite, 'I believe you are missing a lot. I fear you have been misinformed by the adverse publicity and propaganda of our enemies.'

'Those being the neutral worlds you've assimilated, I take

it?' Benny asked. She smiled in response to Straklant's glare. 'Just making sure I'm keeping up.'

'I take it that the reported atrocities, the concentration camps, the so-called alien cleansing are also vicious hyperbole put about by the wanton aggressors whose territory you have assimilated,' Braxiatel said.

Straklant looked at them both for a while before he replied. 'In my opinion, we get a bad press,' he said at last. He held up his hand as Benny made to reply and continued quickly: 'Also, in my opinion, in my personal opinion...' He drew a deep breath and looked from Benny to Braxiatel. 'Which you will appreciate I can only express amongst friends and those I can trust, some of us in the Fifth Axis forces are more, how can I put it – enthusiastic about the campaign than others. A little more extreme in their views and how they carry out their duties.'

'Whereas you just follow orders?' Benny asked.

'You are in the Security Elite,' Braxiatel pointed out. 'Propaganda notwithstanding, they are the ones reputed to have the most extreme and enthusiastic views of all.'

'I am in the Elite,' Straklant confessed. 'And yes, they are the...' He paused, as if unsure whether to continue. 'The worst,' he said at last. 'But understand, please, that my section is in the Elite purely for reasons of administration and management. We're a group charged with sorting out the very problem you have alluded to.'

'I believe I alluded to several,' Braxiatel said. He started counting off on his fingers. 'Let me see now, totalitarianism, genocide...'

'Please!' Straklant interrupted. 'Please, allow me to finish. I am in charge of the Relic Restoration Team. You were right, there is too much acquisition of art and antiques, of archaeological relics without any idea of their worth, or any attempt to keep track of what they are and where they originated.'

'And you're going to put a stop to this acquisition?' Benny asked.

'Well, no.'

'Then, what?'

Straklant gulped. 'It has gone on for too long already. And there are vested interests as I'm sure you realise.'

'So what are you going to do?' Braxiatel asked in a tone that suggested he already knew.

'We're going to catalogue it.'

Nobody said anything for a while. Benny was tempted to laugh at the absurdity of it. But somehow it just didn't seem funny. Eventually she said: 'I'm sorry, but that will help – how?'

Straklant sighed. 'Look,' he said, 'I can't stop what's happening. But I can make sure it's organised and open. Keep track of what goes where. And eventually, who knows, maybe these things will get back to their rightful owners, though that's another argument. But think of it.' He leaned forward, suddenly enthusiastic. 'With the rate the Axis is expanding, what we'll end up with is a comprehensive register of every relic, every artefact, every piece of art of any value and interest in known space. Think of the possibilities. Think of what a research tool that would be.' His eyes were gleaming as he spoke.

'I'm thinking,' Benny said. 'Can't say I'm impressed though. Can't you catalogue stuff without stealing it first?' She smiled as sweetly as she felt able. 'Just a thought.'

'And so you came here,' Braxiatel said, 'thinking that I might condone this?'

Straklant looked embarrassed again. 'Well, there isn't a lot of actual support within the Axis for my work. Apart from getting set up, I have very limited resources. I was thinking you might help fund it.'

There was another long pause, during which Straklant's expression faded from enthusiastic to hopeful. Then from hopeful to crestfallen.

'What you propose,' Braxiatel said at last, 'may be the least worst option available under the circumstances. But I cannot in all honesty condone it or offer any sort of assistance.'

They talked around the subject some more, but without making any progress. Straklant was keen to have their approval and Braxiatel's financial help, and stressed that he was doing what little could be done under the circumstances. Braxiatel insisted that he could not help. And Benny could see both sides of the argument, which did not make it any easier.

Eventually they agreed to differ, and to move on.

'So, with Pettit a dead end,' Braxiatel began.

'And a dead body,' Benny pointed out.

'We turn our attention to what he was after,' Braxiatel went on as if she hadn't spoken.

'Which is?'

'Interesting.' He dimmed the lights and opened a cupboard to reveal a holoprojector. 'We're all ready, so let me show you.'

'You've peeked already,' Benny said accusingly as she turned to see where the image was forming in the middle of the room. 'Haven't you.'

'This isn't the original, of course. That was destroyed long ago. And this is only half of it, of course. It's funny,' Braxiatel went on, 'that I couldn't find a catalogue entry for it. I'm usually pretty meticulous about that sort of thing, but as it is I have absolutely no idea how I came by –'

'Why "only half of it, of course"?' Straklant asked, cutting him off.

'Because of what it is.'

'Has anyone ever told you how infuriating you can be sometimes?' Benny asked.

'Not that I recall,' Braxiatel said. 'Present company excluded of course.' She could hear his smile through the dimly lit room.

The image was complete now – solid and real. In front of them, floating in the air, was the cover of an old notebook. It was dull brown, faded and stained. And it was torn neatly in two down the middle.

'Is that what I think it is?' Straklant asked, his voice husky.

'I haven't a clue, if that helps,' Benny said brightly. 'Do I lose credibility points for that or win on honesty?'

The torn cover swung open to reveal the opening pages – also torn in half. One was a cover page. What remained, the left hand side of the page, read:

Kasagrad Expe
Niall Goram an

The other page was a mass of faded handwriting. Notes were scrawled in the margin, and there were numerous crossings out, amendments and additions. It was practically illegible.

'This,' said Braxiatel, 'according to the extensive checks I've made, is the only existing record of Niall Goram's half of the Doomsday Manuscript.'

Straklant gave a low whistle.

'Looks like my diary,' Benny said. 'Only neater. Call me a Philistine,' she went on as the torn pages continued to turn slowly, 'but what exactly is this charmingly-named Doomsday Manuscript?'

'I doubt if it's anything more than a curiosity actually,' Braxiatel said. 'Possibly even an elaborate hoax.' But he was watching intently as the pages continued to turn. Each was covered in scrawled notes. Occasionally hand-drawn diagrams and even grainy photographs appeared on a page, each torn down the middle.

'I agree,' Straklant said. 'Certainly I don't believe just looking at it will bring about the end of the world.'

'Er,' Benny interjected, 'could we pause it just for a moment, please? You know, while we discuss in just a little more detail this end of the world business.'

'Oh we're quite safe, even if the stories are true,' Braxiatel reassured her. But he paused the animation anyway. The book froze on a discoloured photograph. Like every page, it was ripped down the centre. What was left of it showed a group of three people. No, four – there was another figure in the shadows at the back of the group. They were standing in front of a wall built from huge slabs of sandy stone. Several of the stone slabs had been removed to form an entranceway through the wall, and a passage could be seen inside sloping downwards into the darkness.

'That's why Goram and Lacey split it in half. So that nobody could see the whole manuscript at once,' Straklant was saying.

'Or so the story goes,' Braxiatel agreed.

Benny was only half listening. She was staring at the photograph. It was unsettling. Something about it demanded her attention. She looked carefully at the excavated entranceway, examined the faces of the people standing round it. One of them was torn in two, the right side of his face was missing. Incongruously a huge, bushy moustache extended across the remainder of the man's weather-beaten, smiling face.

Behind him, in the shadows was another figure, leaning casually back against the wall with his arms folded. His face was in shadow and Benny strained to see it more clearly. She leaned to the side, but though the image was three-dimensional what it showed was an old-fashioned flat photograph, so that didn't help. Even so, Benny could feel the bottom of her stomach falling into space as she realised what she was looking at.

'I think you'd better tell me about this manuscript,' she said as she felt the blood drain from her cheeks.

'Of course.' Braxiatel was watching her closely. 'Are you all right?'

'I'm fine,' she said quickly. 'Just tell me. Please.'

'This manuscript, the complete manuscript, purports to be a record of an expedition made by Niall Goram and Matt Lacey to the lost Tomb of Rablev on Kasagrad.' Braxiatel stood up and walked into the hologram. 'This is Goram,' he said jabbing his finger into the face of one of the men in the picture. 'And this is Lacey.'

'And moustachio-man?' Benny asked.

'Don't know, I'm afraid. Local help perhaps.'

'Same for the man behind?'

Braxiatel peered at the shadowy figure. 'Probably. Hadn't noticed him.'

'So where does the doomsday bit come into it?'

'Because if anyone finds and opens the tomb, it's the end of the world,' Straklant said lightly. 'The end of Kasagrad, anyway.'

'As I say,' Braxiatel went on, 'it's just a story. But Kasagrad is rich in antiquities and tombs. Legends develop in such circumstances. The legend of the lost tomb was that Rablev, the Chief Engineer of King Hieronimes, was entombed for crimes against the gods. He offended them, somehow, so much that it was said that if anyone ever found and entered the tomb the gods would destroy the world.'

'When was that?' Benny was sure now.

'Three thousand years ago. Give or take.'

'And the expedition?'

'About four hundred years ago. Hence this rather crude level of imaging.' He waved his hand round inside the photo, stirring up interference patterns as he disturbed the light source.

'So this photograph was taken four hundred years ago?' Benny asked.

Braxiatel nodded and stepped out of the image. 'The age of the document isn't disputed. Only whether they actually found anything at all.'

'They found it by chance,' Straklant said. 'Or so the story goes. They closed it up again and intended to return with a proper expedition.'

'Only they died, of course.'

Benny held up her hand. 'Woah! Why "of course"?' she asked. 'Where did that come from?'

'Because of the curse.'

'Oh yes. Silly me.' She gave what she hoped was a suitably self-deprecating laugh.

'Some sort of wasting disease, as I recall,' Braxiatel

explained. 'And while they were in the final stages, Goram and Lacey agreed to split the manuscript. They couldn't bear to destroy the only record of the Tomb's existence, but they knew that nobody could ever go back there. They believed, actually believed by then, that this was a final warning from the gods and if anyone went back there the world really would come to an end.'

Benny stood up and stretched. 'Well, let's hope they were wrong,' she said. 'I mean if we're going to find this lost tomb.'

'Find it?' Braxiatel laughed. 'I doubt it ever really existed.' He stopped laughing as he noticed her expression. 'You are joking, aren't you? This is just a curiosity. Chances are it's just a story.'

'I think it's more than a curiosity,' Benny said. She was serious, determined. 'I say we go and find out. Let's get the other half of the book, stick it back together and go and look. There are questions here I want answered.'

'Like whether you'll destroy the world?' Braxiatel asked with a wry smile.

'Dale Pettit, and whoever he was working for, obviously thought it was more than a story. Probably after the untold riches and vast treasures that were entombed with Rablev,' Strakland said. 'I vote we go.'

'I didn't even know about the treasures and riches,' Benny said. 'Makes it slightly more tempting, I have to admit.'

'And it will give me the chance to demonstrate how committed I am to doing my job,' Straklant said. 'Doing it with integrity and honesty.'

Braxiatel sighed. 'I have to say that I'm not sure there is any point to this.'

'I'd have thought you'd want to find out what Pettit was after, and why,' Benny said.

'That's why you're determined to go?' Braxiatel's tone suggested he was still not convinced.

'No.' Benny walked into the projection and stood beside the half-man with the impressive moustache. 'I'm going because I want to know how he got to get his picture taken on a secret archaeology expedition four hundred years ago.' She pointed to the figure standing in the shadows.

Braxiatel frowned. 'Let me adjust the brightness and enhance the focus,' he said quietly as he moved to the projector. The figure in the background seemed almost to step forwards, into the light, as the image refocused.

'Who is it?' Straklant asked.

Braxiatel drew in his breath sharply.

There was no doubt about it now. Not that there had ever been for Benny – she knew the stance, the easy way the man was leaning against the wall as if watching rather than being watched. Aloof and amused. 'That,' she said, 'is my ex-husband. Jason Kane.'

Interlude I

He had ordered that the holo-imager be positioned so that it showed the portrait behind his desk. Marshal Raul Kendrick stood in the centre of the imaging area to check that he had a perfect view of both his desk and the huge image.

'Yes,' he told the technician. 'Yes, that will do. How long until the link-up?'

The technician was a small man, balding, rotund and nervous. 'The relay ships will be online in about five minutes, sir.'

'Good.'

'Was there anything else, sir?'

Kendrick considered. 'I don't think so. The computer knows today's frequency code, I assume.'

The technician nodded. 'You will get the right connection, sir, I assure you.'

Kendrick's mouth twisted into an approximation of a smile, the edges of it disappearing beneath his eye patch. 'I wouldn't like to think I was talking to a simulation of General Dench generated to mislead our enemies.'

'No danger of that, sir. I assure you.' The technician's tremulous voice belied his assertion.

But Kendrick had faith in the man. Fear was a great incentive, he had learned. Up to a point of course. Too much fear and a man lost his edge, his judgement. But just the right amount and it was amazing what someone in fear of his life, the lives of his friends, and particularly the lives of his children, could achieve.

After the technician had gone, Kendrick took a few moments to compose himself behind his desk. He opened a folder and spread a few papers out. Field reports, feedback from agents at the front and behind enemy lines. Enough to give the impression he was working hard, but not so much as to suggest he was not in total control of the work. Major Heinman had been dismissed from service because he complained he had too much to do, sent to the glavis mines on Tintinambulus. It was an object lesson well taught.

The holo-imager hummed into life as the datastream flowed into and through it and an image started to form in the air before Kendrick's desk. He looked up, as if caught in the middle of his work. His important work. Expecting to see the craggy, war-torn face of General Immanuel Dench looking down at him with its usual easy superiority.

Kendrick could handle Dench. He might be personal adjutant to the Imperator himself, but he was straightforward enough. Provided you promised to do what was required, and provided you then kept those promises, he played fair. He was a soldier after all. A man of honour.

But the image that formed was not of Dench.

At first, Kendrick thought he was looking into a mirror, that he was seeing a reflection of the portrait on the wall behind his desk. But then the face in front of him blinked. He was facing the Imperator himself. And Kendrick's blood froze in his veins.

Volf Gator, Imperator of the Fifth Axis, was not a large man. If they met in person – which they once had, to Kendrick's unashamed pride – he would reach no higher than Kendrick's shoulder. But now his image towered over his subordinate, his piercing blue eyes boring into the Marshal's conscience. The Imperator's black hair was oiled back across his forehead, and his thin nose was a savage beak as he seemed to lean out of the image towards Marshal Kendrick.

'General Dench has been keeping me informed about developments. About your plan.' The Imperator's voice was quiet and soft. For the moment. 'I thought I might hear from you in person how things are going.' His thin lips twisted into a smile. 'I trust you don't mind.'

'Of course not, Imperator.' Kendrick struggled to keep his voice level. 'I have sent an encrypted data packet to General Dench this morning with the latest report and projections.'

The Imperator's magnified hand waved in the air close to

the chandelier. 'I have little time for such things,' he said. 'And I find that a personal report is always so much more enlightening. You agree, I'm sure.'

'Of course, sir.'

'Excellent, Marshal Kendrick. Most excellent.' The eyes shone as they caught the light at the source of the image. 'By the way, I saw your son yesterday. I had the honour of presenting him with a Platinum Cross for his part in the Galamanus campaign.'

'I'm sure the honour was all his, sir.'

The Imperator nodded slightly, the movement magnified by the size of his projected image looming over the desk. 'A promising career,' he murmured. 'He does his father proud, I'm sure you agree.'

But Kendrick was not so naïve. He knew what the Imperator was really telling him. 'Whatever honour he brings me, it is through his dedication to the Axis, to our Imperator,' he replied stiffly.

The Imperator leaned his head slightly to one side. 'Indeed,' he said. 'But enough of all this.' His eyes gleamed again as he leaned forwards eagerly. 'Tell me how your plan is proceeding. You appreciate the importance to us of the Kasagrad operation, I know. After all, if anything does go wrong, you are the officer closest to the fall-out.' He smiled again, as if amused at his own joke.

Kendrick, for his part, swallowed drily, and tried to smile back. His throat was bone dry by the time he finished his report.

The Imperator listened in silence for ten minutes as Kendrick went through the progress to date.

'And the probability projections for the exercise are still in the ninety-plus range, I see, for all aspects,' he said when Kendrick was finished.

Kendrick nodded. So he had read the latest report after all. But before he could think through the implications of this, before he could decide if he had introduced any discrepancies, the Imperator was speaking again:

'You are confident of the abilities of your agent?'

'Of course,' Kendrick replied automatically.

'And of his loyalty.'

'As of my own.'

The Imperator smiled again. The link was closing, his image fading as the relay ships moved off station and the frequencies changed. 'Then I can hold you wholly responsible,' the Imperator said. 'For the undoubted success of this enterprise,' he added.

But as he sat alone in his office, staring at the space where the Imperator of the Fifth Axis had been, Marshal Raul Kendrick had no illusions about what he had really meant.

3
Trust and Betrayal

Bernice Summerfield's diary. Entry for Wednesday January 2nd 2600.

It's a funny thing, hope. Apart from being generally upset and wobbly about the fact that Jason's gone, I thought I was over it. Well, pretty much. I mean, once someone's been sucked into another dimension you have to resign yourself to the fact that in all probability you're not going to be seeing him again.

In all probability.

Doesn't stop you missing them though. But when there's no hope, there's just the memory. There's the turning to talk to someone who isn't there. Expecting at any moment to see him again but knowing all the time that you won't. Keeping a picture or two handy because you're terrified you might forget what he looks like. It's strange, I can still hear his voice, imagine he's talking to me. But his face, well it's sort of muzzy. I know it as soon as I see it, but I can't conjure it up. Not like his voice. Or the way he stands. Or the way he upsets and infuriates me. Used to...

So, it fades. You get used to it. Life goes on and you make do. The feeling of loss, the hole in your mind, gets smaller.

So it's a funny thing that hope makes it worse.

When I couldn't find that picture the other night, I thought that was it. Time for a clean break. Forget and move on. As if it was somehow 'meant.' And just as I'm resigned to it, just as I know for certain that I can cope, he comes back to haunt me.

I'm pretty sure I'd know if Jason had ever been to Kasagrad and discovered the Lost Tomb of Rablev. He'd have mentioned it. In passing. Just to annoy me and make me envious. And in the picture he looks – well, he looks exactly as I remember him. No, younger, and his hair's grown back to its natural darker brown. And it's messier. But he looks no older. Standing just as he did in the picture I lost. There's a certain symmetry there, I suppose. In fact there's an irony to the whole deal, if you're into that sort of thing. Which, of course, I'm not.

I think Brax understands. Poor old Irving's probably lost more people than I've had hot chocolates. That's why he's let us go. So here I am, pursuing the two loves of my life – an archaeological mystery, and Jason Kane. In the company of a tall, slim, blond guy with piercing blue eyes, an aristocratic manner, a passion for history and relics, and a false hand. Who just happens to be an officer in the most feared army unit in this part of the cosmos. Hey-ho.

The best approach is to concentrate on finding the other half of the manuscript and then the lost tomb, and forget about Jason for now. Until we're in a position to start looking for clues as to where he was. Or is. Only, where Jason's concerned, I always find that the best and most professional

Post-It Note covering the rest of the paragraph:

Blah blah blah blah blah blah blah blah blah blah blah blah blah blah blah blah blah blah blah blah blah blah blah blah blah blah blah blah blah blah blah blah blah blah blah blah blah blah blah blah blah blah blah blah blah de blah blah

Brax managed to dig up some reference to the other half of the manuscript – Lacey's half. Seems it was auctioned off some thirty years or so back when the family needed the dosh. Luckily, it was bought by the grandfather of some collector that Brax actually knows. Though, thinking about it, luck probably isn't really an issue here. I bet he knows every collector who has a collection worth collecting. So we're off to Milo Yendipp's private residence on Habadoss to see if he still has it. And if we can steal a peek at it.

Meanwhile, I've been spending the journey catching up with what my colleague Kolonel Straklant already seems to know: the background to this Lost Tomb thing and the so-called Doomsday Manuscript. I'm always gobsmacked by the way archaeology and melodrama seem to go together. You wouldn't think that grubbing about in the mud, crouched on all fours as often as not until your back aches would get that sort of image, would you? Though now I come to think about it...

Anyway, brief summary to get my own thoughts in order as much as anything:

About three thousand years ago on the planet now called Kasagrad, there was a powerful region also called Kasagrad. Actually, it got so powerful eventually that's how the planet got its name. Now of course it's a strategic island left behind in the midst of the Fifth Axis advance through the Assimilated Territories. Which should make for a fun time when and if we ever get there.

They call it the Time of the Tombs. And one of the Big Figures in the history of the period was the King-Emperor Hieronimes. He had a Chief Engineer called Rablev (as in Lost Tomb of...) who apparently tapped into the very 'power of the gods' and made it available to the people. This 'power' ensured that Kasagrad moved rapidly into the next stages of civilisation and paved the way for its future. Which sounds like a Good Thing generally.

Except that reading between the ancient lines, it seems that Rablev's own ambition was to use his position and the kudos he'd got from his power-thing to usurp Hieronimes and become King-Emperor of all Kasagrad. His big mistake was to let Hieronimes find this out. Result: huge political struggle, which Rablev would have won, except... And here's where it gets a bit messy and confused and fact gets muddled with fiction.

The story goes that the gods grew angry with Rablev for taking their power (a bit like getting miffed at Prometheus for nicking fire, I suppose), and so they visited a terrible vengeance on the people of Kasagrad. No doubt a lot of this is propaganda put about by Hieronimes after the event. But it does seem that the gods poisoned the land so that nothing would grow. There was famine, death, plague... Probably all natural disasters, of course. But in those days there was a divine meaning to everything that Nature did.

So, major loss of credibility for Rablev. Major setback in fact, because everyone who 'tended the power' died of the Curse of the Gods. So far as we can tell, they became sick and then sort of wasted to death as a punishment.

Which gave Hieronimes his excuse. So, to appease the gods, he said, (but really to get rid of Rablev and secure his own position), Hieronimes had Rablev entombed with 'the symbol of his power' whatever that might mean. High 'yuk-factor' here as Rablev might have been ill with god-waste but he was still alive when he got walled up. As, it seems, were most of his friends and family and servants and pets and anyone else who knew him, basically.

Net result, Hieronimes wins on points. Then he has the chronicles and writings either destroyed or amended, and all memory of Rablev and his crime against the gods is blotted from history. The only exception, it seems, being the writings within the tomb itself, which detailed Rablev's crime and his punishment.

Even when the tomb was broken into, since it contained not just the 'power' but also Rablev's personal fortune. The tomb robbers who survived the traps and hazards built into the tomb were captured and executed to preserve the secret... Cue the Curse: It was said that if ever the tomb was disturbed, the gods would again wreak their vengeance on the land... But this time there would be no remission, no redemption: Doomsday.

So there you go.

All of which rather begs the question: if they destroyed all records, how come we know about it? And the answer seems to be that until about four hundred years ago, we didn't. There's some evidence of the famine and plague and all that. But the only direct evidence for any of this is from Goram and Lacey's manuscript. Which to my mind makes it sound about as genuine as The Diary of Jack the Ripper.

Certainly nobody in their right mind would waste any time or effort trying to follow it up. Either the whole thing's a hoax, or we're in danger of bringing about the end of the world.

Actually, there have been times when I've thought that seeing

Jason again is pretty much equivalent to the end of the world. But whatever else it might be, it's a good story.

Which gets me every time.

Milo Yendipp lived with his sister in a large house set in a large field of artificial grass. A taxi-flier from the spaceport dropped Benny and Straklant close to the house before lifting back into the azure sky and skimming away across the high rise buildings and disappearing into the distance.

They found Yendipp waiting for them at the door. He was middle-aged, short and almost bald. His face was lined and his cheeks were as saggy as his stomach. His initial enthusiasm as he greeted them was soon dispelled.

'Milo Yendipp,' he announced. 'You must be Professor Summerfeld.' He stood aside so that they could see the pale, thin woman behind him. 'My little sister, Luci.'

Benny stifled a grin. Luci looked about twice as tall as Milo, her height emphasised by her slim figure. She looked about twenty years younger too, though her good looks and handsome face were marred by fatigue and ill humour. She wore her hair severely short, like a schoolboy. Her eyelids were painted dark blue and her lips were the colour of dried blood.

'Kolonel Daglan Straklant.' He clicked his heels and gave a short bow as he introduced himself.

Yendipp and his sister froze. 'Kolonel?' Yendipp queried, his voice trembling slightly and his face pale.

'He's with the Fifth Axis,' Benny said lightly, watching for their reaction. 'Just along for the ride. I hope that isn't a problem.'

'No.' Yendipp gave an obviously forced smile. 'No problem at all.' Behind him his sister turned and ran into the dark interior of the house.

There was a buffet laid out in the main reception room. Luci stayed only long enough to pour drinks. Benny hadn't heard her utter a word.

63

'Your sister seems a bit...' She struggled to find a tactful word. 'Distracted,' she decided.

'I apologise.' Yendipp sounded like that was the last thing he was doing. He fixed Straklant with a stare that seemed almost incompatible with his deep set, piggy eyes. 'We were only expecting you, Professor. More guests mean more work. I'm sure you understand.'

'Of course,' Benny said. She felt awkward and embarrassed and wished she knew what was really going on.

Straklant by contrast seemed amused and at ease. 'I take it that neither of you has any love for the Fifth Axis,' he said lightly. 'I apologise if you take exception to my presence.' He sounded as contrite as Yendipp had.

'It would be wrong to take exception to someone we didn't know,' Yendipp said. 'Please forgive Luci. She has only recently been widowed.'

It was a strangely formal and apparently unsympathetic way of putting it, but Benny could feel for the woman suddenly. Even before the exchange that followed.

'My condolences to her,' Straklant said.

'I'm not sure she will accept them,' Yendipp said, his voice suddenly hard and determined. He pulled himself to his full, not terribly impressive height and stared up at the tall blond officer. 'Her husband died on Frastus Minima.'

Straklant blinked. This obviously meant something to him. 'Ah,' he said, and sighed. 'That was an unfortunate business.'

'That,' said a voice from behind them, 'was mass murder.'

They all swung round, to see Luci standing in the doorway. She was holding a tray with more food on it. She avoided their gaze and took it to the table. The plates clattered as she slammed down the tray.

Her brother took a tentative step towards her, his hand sneaking out nervously. 'Luci, Luci,' he murmured soothingly.

'Forgive me,' Straklant said gently, 'but despite what you may have heard in the media, the propaganda, nobody really knows what happened there.'

She did not answer. She leaned forward over the table, absolutely still.

'Even I don't know,' Straklant went on. 'After all, how could I? I wasn't there.'

She spun round at this and Benny could see the fire and emotion in her eyes. 'I was,' she said. Her voice was tense and raddled with nerves and anger. 'I know exactly what happened. I saw them die.' Her heels ricocheted off the hard wood floor as she left.

The atmosphere was somewhat less tense by the time that Yendipp, Benny and Straklant moved to Yendipp's conference room.

Even so, Yendipp prefaced their discussions by making it clear he was helping Benny, and not Straklant.

'Do you still have the other half of the manuscript?' Straklant demanded.

Yendipp ignored him.

'We were wondering,' Benny said politely, 'if you still have the other half – Lacey's half – of the Doomsday Manuscript.'

Yendipp considered. He tucked his shirt in. He was always tucking his shirt in. 'No,' he said. 'No, I don't.'

'Then we're wasting our time,' Straklant said and got to his feet.

'You are free to leave as soon as you wish,' Yendipp told him. 'But I have assembled some information that I think Professor Summerfield might find of interest. From what little I have left, or can access from extant records.'

Straklant sat down again. 'Go on then.'

Benny smiled at Yendipp. 'He means, "thank you,"' she said. She shot a glare at Straklant. 'Don't you.'

'Of course,' he conceded. 'Forgive me. I...' He hesitated, swallowed, shook his head. 'I find it difficult sometimes to accept the responsibility and weight of the actions of some of my colleagues and compatriots. Forgive me for that too.'

Yendipp sighed. 'I am sorry also,' he said. 'It is difficult at such times. I have no wish to mete out the same intolerance to a group of people as I see them display towards others.' He looked at Benny, and she could see the deep sadness in his eyes. 'As soon as we do that, we are no better than...' He broke off and shook his head.

'No better than I am?' Straklant prompted, the anger obvious in his voice.

'That is not what I meant,' Yendipp said. He held up his pudgy hands. 'Please, I think we both have a good idea of what each of us is trying to say. And we both share the difficulty and the pain in bringing ourselves to say it. Let's not quibble about the clumsy way we try to phrase our thoughts and feelings.'

The facilities were not as impressive as Braxiatel's. What Yendipp had to show was displayed on a screen at the far end of the room rather than hovering in the air in front of them. But since most of the material was old and two-dimensional that did not detract from it.

As he talked them through it, Yendipp's enthusiasm grew. Before long all trace of resentment and sadness was gone from his voice. 'This is Niall Goram, just a few weeks before the expedition.'

A jerky, faded film clip played across the screen. It showed a young man in obvious good health kicking a ball to a small boy.

'That's his oldest son, Rickard.'

The clip froze on Goram's face – young, vigorous, and happy. The image faded and was replaced by what looked like an old man. The skin was almost translucent and blotchy, the eyes sunken and the hair was shrivelled, white and thinning. The camera pulled back and the old man began to walk – stiffly, slowly, with obvious effort and pain.

'Who's that?' Straklant asked.

'That too is Niall Goram. After the expedition.'

'Decades after, by the look of him,' Benny said.

'By the look of him,' Yendipp agreed. 'In fact this film was taken just four months – four months,' he emphasised, 'after

66

the one you first saw.'

Benny gasped. 'You're kidding!'

Yendipp shook his head. 'Now look at Matt Lacey,' he said. 'Only stills, I'm afraid.

The contrast was every bit as marked. Only the eyes gave any hint that the two pictures that Yendipp displayed side by side were the same person. Again, one was young, healthy, happy. The other was a degenerate old man – emaciated with discoloured skin and almost completely bald.

'Little wonder,' Yendipp said quietly, 'that they both came to believe absolutely in the authenticity of the curse before they died. Little wonder that they agreed that whatever they found in that tomb must remain undisturbed for all eternity.'

'How rapidly did this happen?' Straklant asked.

'From what I can tell, it was extremely rapid. Once it started.' Yendipp adjusted the lights and the dual faces of Matt Lacey faded on the screen. 'When they first got back they were enthusiastic, excited. Determined to return and excavate their find properly and professionally. It seems they rather stumbled across it. They explored, disturbed very little, took notes and then sealed it up again. I imagine they could not believe their luck.'

Benny gave a humourless laugh. 'Not quite the sort of luck they thought. So you think they really did find something? It's not just a story?'

Yendipp gestured to the screen. 'You saw them. That doesn't just happen by chance. And not to both of them. They were terrified and they were dying. Oh yes,' he said. 'They found something. I have no doubt that they found the Lost Tomb of Rablev and went inside. And they had no doubt that to open it again would mean the end of the world.'

'So they split the manuscript, to prevent anyone else finding it,' Straklant said.

Yendipp nodded. 'Each family kept half. Our mutual friend Irving Braxiatel tells me that he now has Goram's half. My grandfather purchased the Lacey half when it came up for auction a while ago. Sadly, I found myself in a similar financial situation to its original owners and was forced to part with it as well.'

'The curse?' Benny asked with a smile.

'Loss of estates and their income within the Assimilated Territories,' Yendipp said. He did not look at Straklant. 'I sold it on just in time. Otherwise the Fifth Axis would have taken it as they took everything else I valued.'

'And where is it now?' Straklant asked. There was no trace of sympathy or regret in his voice this time. Only eagerness.

'It was purchased by an anonymous buyer,' Yendipp said. He fixed Benny with a stare. 'I wish I could tell you more,' he said levelly.

She nodded, catching his meaning.

'But surely you kept a copy,' Straklant said. 'That's just common sense.'

Yendipp shook his head. 'The value of the manuscript derives from the fact that there are no copies. It is unique.'

'But even so.'

'No, Kolonel Straklant. The agreement was that the purchaser would get the only existing copy.' Yendipp was sounding distinctly aggrieved at Straklant's questioning.

'And it didn't occur to you that they wouldn't know if you kept a duplicate?' Straklant was both incredulous and angry.

'It doesn't matter if they know or not,' Yendipp snapped back. 'I would know. I gave my word, and I keep it. That's what trust and honour are all about, but perhaps you wouldn't know that.'

They stared at each other, each breathing heavily. Straklant was poised and composed, only his flushed face betraying his anger.

'Let's just accept that there is no copy, shall we?' Benny suggested. 'I think it would be a help if we could part reasonably amicably, hmm?'

Yendipp lowered his gaze before Straklant did. 'Yes, of course,' he mumbled. 'I do apologise. I accept that many collectors would indeed have kept a copy, but I confess that my priorities lie elsewhere.'

'I do have one question you may be able to answer,' Benny said, partly by way of changing the subject. Partly. It was the question she had wanted to ask all along. 'Is there any record, so far as you know, of anyone else going with Lacey and Goram on the expedition?'

'Anyone else?' The very suggestion seemed to surprise Yendipp.

'We have a picture of two other men with them at the site,' Straklant said. 'We assume it is the site anyway.'

'From Goram's part of the manuscript?'

Benny nodded. 'Have you come across any reference to them having help?'

Yendipp shook his head. 'No,' he said slowly. 'None that I recall. And I would recall, I'm sure.'

Benny nodded. She believed him. But it was hard to mask her disappointment. 'So the name Jason Kane means nothing to you?' she asked.

'I'm sorry,' he said. 'It means nothing at all.'

To Straklant's obvious annoyance, Benny offered to let Yendipp see the Goram half of the document. But he declined, with sadness in his voice. He could probably tell them little from it, he said, and it would merely bring back memories he had no wish to rekindle. Not now. Again there was something deep within his eyes as he spoke to Benny. She knew she needed to talk to him alone.

It was easy to get Straklant out of the way. They had called for a taxi-flier to take them to the spaceport, and Benny asked Straklant to wait outside and keep a lookout for it.

'I think he may open up a bit if you're not here,' she whispered to him. 'No offence.'

'None taken,' he murmured back. 'And I think you're right.' He shrugged. 'After all, I can only apologise so many times.'

Benny squeezed his arm and smiled. Her guess was that he was brash and brusque and rude because underneath he was embarrassed and ashamed.

'I suppose you'll have to tell your colleague,' Yendipp said when they were alone. 'But I cannot bear to tell him myself. I'm sorry.' He stared at the floor, his hands twisting together in front of him as he spoke in a low voice.

'I won't tell him anything you don't want me to,' Benny assured him. 'You can trust me, you know.'

He looked up at that. 'Yes,' he said, 'I believe I can.' He came the closest to a smile she had seen since they arrived.

'So,' Benny hazarded, 'what do you want to tell me?' And to show that she knew she could trust him, she added: 'I know you didn't keep a copy of the manuscript.'

'No, I didn't. But I do know who bought it.'

'I thought you said they were anonymous.'

Yendipp smiled again, more fully this time. 'Some people find it difficult to remain anonymous,' he said. 'The buyer was Munroe Hennessy.'

Benny whistled. 'Well,' she said, 'I suppose finding him won't be a problem. Though getting to see him might.'

'Mention my name,' Yendipp offered. 'If it helps.' He shrugged.

'Thanks,' Benny told him. 'For everything.' She shook his hand. 'And thank your sister too. I know our visit wasn't easy for her.'

His eyes were watering as he opened the door for her. 'Most nights,' he said, almost to himself, 'I hear her crying in her sleep.'

Benny hesitated in the doorway. 'Thanks for all your help,' she said again. There was not much else she could say.

'What sad people.'

The taxi-flier was waiting. Straklant keyed the passenger door for Benny to get in. He was about to follow when he seemed to change his mind.

'Yes,' he said thoughtfully. 'Yes, they are sad. Did you get anything useful?'

'I think so.' Benny grinned as she settled herself into the

seat. 'I know who bought the manuscript.'

Straklant returned her smile. Then he turned away from the flier.

'Where are you going?'

'I said you can only apologise so many times,' he called back. 'But once more might help.' He smiled at her. 'Especially as we're leaving.'

She watched as Yendipp opened the door. She could not hear what they said, but after a few moments, both men stepped inside the house. The door swung slowly shut behind them.

'What a nice man,' Benny murmured.

Yendipp was nervous. He was sweating and Straklant could smell it.

'What was it you wanted to say to me?' Yendipp asked.

'I wanted to apologise. That's all.'

'Oh?' There was a flicker of relief in the fat man's eyes.

'Yes. You see, I lied.'

The relief changed to puzzlement. 'Lied? I don't understand. What about?'

'About offering my condolences to your sister.' Straklant smiled at him. 'About finding it difficult to accept responsibility for the actions of my colleagues.' His smile widened into a grin. 'About wanting your forgiveness.' The skin on his face stretched tight as he grinned wider, so that his face was almost skull-like. 'And you lied to me.'

Yendipp was gaping, shaking his head, looking round. The smell of his sweat was stronger now. 'I... No, I –'

'About how the Fifth Axis took everything you have,' Straklant prompted. His voice was quiet, silky-smooth. 'Oh,' he added, 'and I lied about Frastus Minima as well.'

'You know what happened?' Yendipp gulped. He looked round again.

'Your sister doesn't seem to be around,' Straklant said. 'A pity. You see I was there, on Frastus. I commanded the infantry division that sanitized the planet.' He raised his hand, holding it in front of Yendipp's face, fingers extended.

'I may even have killed her husband myself.' With his other hand, his right hand, he took hold of the tip of the index finger. 'I certainly hope so.' He pulled. And the finger came free, lifting away to reveal a glinting spike of metal inside. A drop of clear liquid glistened on the point.

Yendipp took a step backwards, his hand clutching at his chest suddenly. His face frozen.

'There, there,' Straklant murmured as he moved closer. 'Have we got a poorly heart?' He levelled his hand, the spike extended towards Yendipp. 'Now, let's have a look at that.'

The spike jabbed into Yendipp's hand as he continued to clutch at his chest. He cried out and jerked it free.

'Does it hurt?' Straklant asked in mock surprise. 'Well, we'll have to do something about that, then won't we?'

Straklant thrust his left hand forward again. 'Of course,' he said, his voice level, conversational, 'the poison will already be killing you. But it does take a while.' The stiletto cut through Yendipp's shirt and into his chest. 'And I am in rather a hurry, I'm afraid.'

A spray of blood – almost a mist it was so fine – erupted from Yendipp's chest. Straklant had been expecting it and stepped back to avoid being caught. As he drew out the spike, the mist became viscous liquid pumping out and down Yendipp's torso, soaking his already sweat-sodden shirt.

'No hard feelings,' Straklant said amicably as he turned away. Behind him he heard the gasping retch that was Yendipp's final attempt at speech. Then the body collapsing to the floor. Kolonel Daglan Straklant of the Fifth Axis Security Elite clicked his tongue, sighed, and left.

Benny waited until he was settled and the flier was lifting off before she asked: 'Okay?'

'Fine.' Straklant seemed relaxed and at ease.

'Can't have been easy,' Benny said. She shifted slightly closer to him on the seat.

'You'd be surprised.' He smiled at her, making her aware

that he knew she had moved.

'Did he thank you?' she asked. 'For making the effort?'

Straklant eased himself slightly closer to Benny. 'Oh yes,' he said. 'From the bottom of his heart.'

4
Lights, Cameras

Bernice Summerfield's diary. Entry for Thursday January 3rd 2600.

Since Munroe Hennessy is renowned for valuing his privacy, we knew we'd never get an appointment to see him. So we just turned up. Sometimes the direct and simple approach really is the most successful (but don't tell Brax!).

So there we were, landing our rented mini-shuttle on a private asteroid, half expecting to be blown out of the sky by some local defence grid. I mean, you begin to wonder whether you should have come. Anyway, we signalled that we'd come to discuss the Doomsday Manuscript (direct and simple, remember?), and got landing clearance.

I was never a big fan. Not one of the teenage swooners. But I did catch some of his holo-vids a while ago. I get a bit muddled over dates, so I was expecting Hennessy to be pretty much as he was in those – dashing, debonair, perfectly-coiffed, handsome, tall… Very much the screen idol. Star quality, and all that. You know – you'll have seen the vids. I suppose I knew he hadn't done any acting for a while. Didn't realise it was over thirty years though!

So I was a bit surprised when the docking tube door opened and he was there to greet us. In his wheelchair. He must be pushing ninety, and not in the best of health. His hair, what's left of it, is white now. His skin's gone sort of mottled and sunk round his face so you can see the outline of the cheek bones, but then it's all saggy round the mouth. His hands are clawed with arthritis, and his voice is assisted by something that makes him sound like he's talking through a piece of kitchen equipment. A cheese grater maybe.

And talking of kitchen equipment, Hennessy's nurse, Fedora Bronsan, has a face that I think was modelled on a meat cleaver. Sharp, hooked nose, pinched features. She's tall and thin as a fish slice. She has that sort of tone that makes it sound like she's deigning to talk to you and struggling to maintain her dignity as she does so.

Anyway, once the introductions were done, then the misunderstandings started. Often the way.

'The Doomsday Script,' Hennessy said in that grating voice. 'You have a draft with you?'

'Er?' I said. Seemed like a good response to me.

He started doing excited little circles in his chair. The motor whines like a food mixer. You can tell I'm ready for dinner here, can't you. 'I shall want script approval of course,' he said.

'Of course,' Bronsan echoed. Like it was up to her.

'Why not,' I said. Straklant was giving me an 'I don't understand either' look by now. So I smiled and shrugged.

'What is it about?' Hennessy demanded.

'About?' I figured it was best just to do the parrot for the moment.

'Drama, tragedy, comedy?' Bronsan snapped.

'Comedy,' I said.

'Drama,' Straklant said.

'Well, it's a bit of a mixture really,' I said.

'And what studio did you say you were from?' Bronsan asked.

'Fifth Axis Pictures,' Straklant said smoothly. I think he cottoned on before I did actually. He's pretty sharp. 'We've recently made some acquisitions.' He smiled at me as he said it. But I didn't smile back.

'And I shall be playing the lead?' Hennessy asked. 'Excellent, excellent,' he went on quickly. In case we really had thought it was a question.

'It's based on a true story,' I said as we followed him down the corridor. 'In fact, that's why we thought of you. Ideal casting. You get to play the lead, and help with the actual research. Provide vital documents.'

The walls of the corridor – actually, the walls of every room – were covered with Munroe Hennessy memorabilia. Munrobelia? There were still holo-frames in the alcoves of what I suppose are famous scenes and tableaux from his work. Lobby cards

76

hanging in frames. Various awards and certificates on display. Sad really.

Not the achievement, what he was. That's great. But seeing this pathetic, wasted little figure wheeling past a holographic image of how he once was – seeing the contrast like that... It reminded me of the before and after pictures of Goram and Lacey. There's no way this guy is making a come back. Not unless he's taking the title role in When We Dead Awaken.

I paused by one of the tableaux. To be polite as much as anything, I guess. That's when I first noticed the cameras. There was one at the side of the scene. I thought it was part of the scene at first. Till I knocked into it and realised it was real, not part of the projection.

They're all over the place. Old holo-imaging cameras. Single-lens jobbies like they used in the old days (the Munroe Hennessy days). They're huge great things compared with what they use now. Almost up to my shoulder, and heavy. They're mounted on a hydraulic rod set into a base that has castors fixed under it so they can be moved along. Quite sinister actually.

There was even one in here, in my bedroom. But I didn't fancy the way it looked at me – like the eyes of portraits, its lens seemed to follow you round the room. So I pushed it outside into the corridor. Facing away from the door.

Got to go now. We're discussing our 'movie' and Hennessy's comeback over dinner. Actually, we're hoping to discuss how we need his half of the Doomsday Manuscript before we can complete the final draft of the shooting script. Bronsan said half an hour and I asked Joseph to let me know when time was up. I don't know why I bothered to bring him – away from a direct link into Braxiatel's scheduling systems he's just a smart egg-timer. With the emphasis on egg-timer. Come to think of it, that's not much different from when he is hooked in.

My stomach alarm's going off now too. Goodness only knows when I last ate.

There were four of the cameras in the dining room. One in each corner, dispassionate glass eyes watching the meal. The lighting was uncomfortably bright, provided by arc lights suspended from the high ceiling. Despite this, there were candles on the table, their flickering flames struggling to be seen.

As Benny had suspected, dinner was hardly a lavish affair. But at least there was a passable red wine to wash down the salad and cold meats arranged on silver platters across the polished wooden table. In fact, looking round, she decided that only the food was cheap. She lifted a heavy silver fork and pointed it at Hennessy. 'Nice place you have here.'

Hennessy was in his wheelchair, as ever, at the head of the table. He seemed to have trouble eating, and Fedora Bronsan had to serve him his food and cut it into bite-sized pieces.

Benny returned her fork to what seemed to be a root vegetable. It tasted of practically nothing. Opposite her, Straklant was hacking his way through a hunk of meat. Benny could see one of the cameras over his shoulder. She gave it a theatrical grin – all teeth. Straklant caught her eye and smiled back, misunderstanding.

Fedora Bronsan took her seat next to Benny. 'We like it here,' she said. 'Though of course there will be travel involved in the production.'

'Of course,' Benny said through a mouthful of something green and stringy.

'You were telling us about the script,' Hennessy ground out.

'Well, as I say it's based on a true story.' Benny put down her knife and fork, grateful for an excuse to stop eating and let her jaw get its strength back. 'And we thought we'd base it on the Doomsday Manuscript. Since you are the owner of one half of it, we thought that would be –'

Bronsan dropped her cutlery. Hennessy drew a deep rasping breath of surprise and shock.

'– a good wheeze,' Benny finished. 'Sorry,' she said quickly. 'I meant, like, fun. You know?'

Looking at their faces, fun seemed at best to be a distant memory to them.

'You do have the Doomsday Manuscript?' Straklant asked sharply. 'It is of course essential to the script development.'

'And the pre-publicity,' Benny added. 'Gives it a very marketable angle, having you involved both within the narrative and in developing it.'

Hennessy was sitting absolutely still, staring down at his lap. For a moment Benny worried he might have died of shock, but then his electronically-aided voice said: 'I acquired the manuscript some years ago. I was not aware that anyone knew I had it.'

'We have very talented researchers,' Straklant assured him.

'Since you know something of the history and legend of the Doomsday Manuscript, you'll agree it makes a cracking story,' Benny said. She took a swig of wine. 'It'll be huge,' she said grandly. 'Really... big.' She crossed her fingers under her napkin.

'The Doomsday Manuscript,' Bronsan said slowly. 'Yes. Yes, that could work.' She looked at Benny, a hint of appreciation in her face. 'I begin to see the possibilities. The dashing vid star who unwittingly comes into possession of half the manuscript is attacked by the evil villainess who wishes to steal it.'

'A chase through his mansion,' Hennessy said. 'Casting will be important.'

'Absolutely,' Benny agreed quickly. 'Who do you think would be up to playing the hero then?' She almost choked as she caught Bronsan's expression and her sharp look.

Benny took a gulp of wine. 'Just kidding. It's the villainess part we need to be careful with I guess.' She shot a look at Straklant, hoping for help. But he was leaning back in his chair, grinning at her. The camera behind was equally unhelpful.

Benny frowned. Since Straklant had moved, the camera should surely be obscured. But it still stared back at her over his shoulder.

'I may need a double,' Hennessy rasped. 'For some of the more demanding stunts.'

'You're telling me!' Benny was still frowning at the camera. Her response was automatic. She coughed, and smiled. 'You're telling me,' she said again, 'that you think we have something here? We might be able to tempt you out of retirement?' She tried to sound hopeful, enthusiastic. Convinced.

'We shall need to see your half of the Doomsday Manuscript, of course,' Straklant put in. He leaned forward again, smiling. 'To make it workable.' Was it Benny's imagination, or had the camera moved forwards slightly as he did?

'Tomorrow,' Hennessy said. 'I grow tired. Tomorrow we shall look at the manuscript and see what is possible.'

'Great,' Benny said. 'Triff.' She leaned across with her glass of wine, and was surprised that Hennessy immediately raised his own glass, leaned forward, and allowed her to clink her glass on his.

'To a successful project,' he said. 'It will be good to get back into the swing of things.'

The phrase sounded strange in the electronic voice. The notion of this wheelchair-bound husk of a man getting into the swing of anything seemed strange to Benny as well. She glanced at Straklant, but he kept his expression neutral.

'I must say, I am heartened by developments so far,' Bronsan said.

Benny turned to find the woman was actually smiling at her. 'Good,' Benny said. 'Provided we get that secondary casting sorted out.'

'Oh believe me,' Bronsan said, 'that won't be a problem.' She was looking at Hennessy now, her face seemed to soften, her eyes deepen. 'Not when the agencies learn that Munroe Hennessy is to come out of retirement.'

'Yes, well, talking of retiring,' Benny said, 'reminds me that I'm quite tired as well. After the journey.'

'We'll resume our contract negotiations tomorrow then,' Bronsan said.

'That sounds good,' Straklant replied. 'And we can see the

Doomsday Manuscript as well.' It wasn't asked as a question.

'Of course,' Hennessy said. 'And I can look over the current draft of your script.'

Straklant and Benny exchanged glances. ''Night, then,' she said and drained her wine. 'By the way,' she added as she stood up,' what was that green stringy stuff?'

'It's Vendolusian plankton. Quite a delicacy,' Hennessy said, his wheelchair pulling back from the table, then angling and coming round towards Benny. 'It is also quite poisonous.'

Benny froze. 'Oh?'

She saw Straklant's eyes narrow. He was standing too.

'Oh yes. Until part-digested by the Vendolusian pond squwelch.'

Benny felt hot suddenly. 'Ah.'

'I'm glad I didn't have any,' Straklant said. 'Tell me, how do they...?' His voice dropped away in a similar manner to Benny's stomach.

'The local farmers catch them when they've fed,' Fedora Bronsan said. 'Then they force their fingers down the creature's throat to induce it to –'

The feeling had returned to Benny's stomach now. But it wasn't going to stay there. 'Vomit!' she gasped, only partly by way of finishing Bronsan's statement. Then she ran from the room.

She had no idea how long she had slept. Not long enough, she decided as she turned over and tried to get back to sleep.

That was when Benny heard the noise from out of the darkness. A loud click. Suddenly she was awake. She sat up and peered across the room.

It was inky black. But there was a light switch by the head of the bed. The blackness receded as the lights came up. Benny looked around. She could see nothing amiss. It was a small room – plain and functional with no windows. There was a desk against one wall with a local-access terminal on it. It didn't work, though. She had tried to get into Hennessy's archive system to see if he had a backup copy of the Doomsday Manuscript in there. But she couldn't even get a logon screen. Maybe it really didn't work. Or maybe they'd disconnected it for her benefit.

Satisfied that nothing was amiss, Benny turned the lights out again and lay down. Strange, she could have sworn that the clicking sound came from the direction of the door. A click. She yawned. Almost as if –

She slammed her hand against the light switch and was out of bed and across the room before they were fully lit.

The door was locked. If she peered into the slit between door and frame she could see the deadbolt. Remote-activated. And she had no key. She sat on the floor, pulling Jason's old shirt close about her. The trick was, she decided, to treat this as an intellectual exercise – a puzzle – rather than panic. Yes, that was best.

With a sob of frustration she crawled rapidly across to her rucksack, picked it up and shook everything out on to the floor. Surely there was something here that might help. Something with which she could force the door.

'Ouch!'

The squeak of surprise and pain was accompanied by the sound of a heavy ball bouncing and rolling along the floor. It stopped as the sphere rose unsteadily into the air.

'You might activate me before throwing me around, Professor Summerfield,' Joseph said.

'Joseph!' She could have hugged him. Or rather, it. 'Oh I'm glad I brought you. I need your help.'

'Of course, Professor. I am at your service.'

'Good. How are you at locks?'

'Locks?' He sounded surprised.

'Door locks, specifically.'

Joseph bobbed towards the door and hovered close by. 'I do detect the residual energy from a carrier activation wave signal for a remote-triggered deadbolt locking system.' Incredibly, he sniffed. 'Probably a Jensson-Armitage from that sort of profile.'

Benny almost laughed with relief. 'Oh thank goodness. Open it will you?'

'Er, open it?' There was a nervous hesitancy in his tone.

Benny's inclination to laugh was fading. 'Yes, open it. Please.'

'I can't, I'm afraid, Professor.'

'Can't? What do you mean, you can't? You knew exactly what it was, didn't you?'

Joseph bobbed about in an agitated manner. 'I know what a black hole is and what it looks like,' he said, voice quavering. 'But that doesn't mean I can do anything about it.' He spun round and described a figure of eight in the air. 'I'm sure you understand, Professor,' he added after a pause.

'Oh yes,' she told him bitterly. 'I understand. You're useless, that's what I understand. All mouth and no trousers.'

'All ball, actually,' Joseph said.

'I think that about sums it up,' Benny agreed. 'You're useless. As useless as…' She walked round the room trying to think of something that was useless enough to make a valid comparison. She stopped in front of the desk. 'As useless as this terminal,' she decided, giving it a slap.

Joseph floated over, as if to inspect the artefact with which he had so much in common. 'That is not useless,' he said in a tone of admonishment. 'It provides access to the local data archive as well as a direct link to the security systems and integrated editing suite.'

'Joseph,' Benny said firmly, 'it doesn't. It does nothing. Look.' She pulled out the datapad and clattered her fingers over it. 'Nothing. Zip. Zilch. Useless.' She shoved the datapad away again. 'How do you know what it used to be connected to anyway?'

'It still is,' Joseph said. 'Only the datapad is disconnected from the system.'

Benny took a deep breath. 'Well, as before, the point I'm making is the same. In its current state, this system is useless. Isn't it.'

Since it wasn't a question, she did not expect an answer. But Joseph gave her one: 'No,' he said. 'All you need, if I may make so bold, is an alternative interface system.'

'Such as?' Not that she cared.

'Well,' Joseph's voice had a hint of pride in it along with the nasal superiority now, 'such as myself.' As he spoke, the screen flickered into life and an image began to form. 'I can interface with the systems directly, as my calendar management facility matches the one on the mainframe. Normally, I should be locked out of other areas, but the security systems on this database are rather lax.' He made a few tut-tut noises and bobbed around the screen.

Benny was hardly listening. She was watching the screen. 'What is this?' she asked.

'It is a Thorland Data Access –'

'No, I mean this.' She jabbed her finger at the screen. 'What we're watching.'

'Oh.' Joseph bobbed closer. 'It's a video-playback feed from the editing suite, whatever that might be. Something somebody cut together this evening judging by the time stamp. From internal security feeds. It looks like dinner.'

It did look like dinner, Benny thought. It was also very different. Benny herself, Straklant, Fedora Bronsan and Munroe Hennessy were all seated round the table, just as they had been. The same table. The same dinner, the same candles. But the candles provided the only flickering, moody light. The room now had a low, painted ceiling where the arc lights had hung. There was no sign of the cameras round the table, though the angle of the picture suggested that one of them had provided it.

The biggest discrepancy, the most obvious change, was Munroe Hennessy, Rather than hunched frail and weak in his wheelchair, he was sitting on a large chair. His hair was dark and perfectly brushed. His face was young and vigorous, his eyes alive and intense. His body was athletic and honed. He looked as if he had just stepped out of one of the holograms of how he had been fifty years ago.

'Can you get me sound on this?' Benny asked.

In reply she heard Hennessy's voice – the smooth, deep

voice from his most impressive performances. 'So, Professor Summerfield,' he was saying, 'you are after my Doomsday Manuscript.'

The angle switched, so that the image framed Benny and Hennessy. The outline of Straklant's shoulder was just visible at the edge of the shot. As Benny watched she saw herself raise her hand and point something at Hennessy. But it wasn't a fork. It was a small and brutal-looking handgun.

'You do have the Doomsday Manuscript?' Straklant's voice asked sharply from out of shot. 'It is of course essential.'

There was a slight flicker, an edit she realised, and Benny turned towards the camera. She grimaced, baring her teeth in what might well have been a menacing threat. 'Thinking of retiring?' she said. It sounded like a threat. Her lips did not quite synch with the speech.

The shot changed again – to a view from the other side of the table showing Straklant as he said: 'We shall need your half of the Doomsday Manuscript.'

Then a close-up of Hennessy – defiant and determined. 'Never!'

Back to the view of Benny and Hennessy. Benny thrust out her hand towards Hennessy, as he leaped to his feet and lashed out at her, the action blurring as it had been speeded up. His hand caught hers, but no wine glasses chinked – the gun flew from her grip and clattered away. Close to the camera, Straklant got to his feet, blotting out the view.

The next angle was from the doorway as Benny ran from the room, one hand to her mouth, as if to escape. Straklant was already starting after her as the picture on the screen faded out.

'End of file,' Josepeh said apologetically.

'You know,' Benny said, tapping her fingers against her teeth, 'I may have got through a few glasses of wine, but that isn't quite how I remember the evening panning out.'

Joseph coughed. 'It looked like a fade to black to me.'

Benny ignored him. She was puzzled and worried. If Hennessy wanted to muck around with holo-video footage in an attempt to recapture his lost youth, that was fine. But why lock her in her room while he did it? 'Are there any other files there in the same area of storage?'

'In that folder, there is just one. It is called Storyboard Sequences.'

'Can you show it?' As Joseph rose and spun above the monitor, Benny sucked in her cheeks. 'It's a pity he didn't add in some useful insert shots of his half of the Doomsday Manuscript,' she mused. 'If you could download that into your local memory, we'd at least have something to show for all this. Whatever this is,' she added as a picture appeared on the screen.

It was a relatively crude, black and white sketch. It showed an angular, inked woman with short shaded hair who might just have been Benny running from the dining room. After a moment, the image faded and another took its place – this time sketch-Benny was in her room, scooping up her rucksack. An arrow showed how her arm swung down to grab the straps.

In the next picture she was leaving the room at a run. And in the next, racing along a corridor, with a stick-like representation of Munroe Hennessy running after her. And so it went on.

Benny watched in silence as her sketched-self was pursued through Hennessy's mansion. Straklant, as far as she could tell, joined her and the tables were turned for a while as he had a gun.

But then, in a flurry of drawings, Hennessy seemed to win a fight and get control of the gun. Straklant was left on the floor, lying in a dark pool of ink.

There was another brief chase. Then the final image: Benny against a wall, a knife in her hand. And Hennessy in an heroic pose, levelling the gun.

By this time Benny had her rucksack packed again. If and when she got the chance she was not going to hang around to find out how they intended to get their footage. 'In you go,' she said to Joseph as she grabbed him out of the air and bundled him in with her dirty socks.

86

The screen faded again to black. Then the door clicked open.

Outside, in the corridor, the camera that Benny had pushed out of her room was waiting, facing her. The camera she had angled so it pointed away from the door. The lens rotated slightly as it focused on her. Waited for her to run.

5
Action!

Benny edged carefully round the camera, slinging her rucksack over her shoulder as she moved. The camera was large and heavy, mounted on castors. It did not seem to be connected to anything, but the top half swung round to follow her as she moved. Again the lens rotated, keeping her in its sights.

She backed away down the corridor. Straklant's room was a little further along. If she could get there safely, then at least she wouldn't be alone. Only when she was well away from the camera, only when she was sure that she could beat it to the room no matter how fast it moved, did Benny turn and run.

Straklant's door, like Benny's, was half open. She guessed it had opened when her own had. The lights were on inside, and she could see that the bed had been slept in. But there was no sign of Straklant. Benny glanced back down the corridor, and saw that the camera was slowly moving after her. Its castors were silent, and it seemed to glide over the smooth floor, its eye-lens staring intently at her.

She meant to call out, to see if Straklant was in the room, but her voice stuck in her throat as she crept cautiously inside. She was torn between the urge to run, and the fear of not knowing what had happened here.

As soon as she was inside she realised her mistake. Behind the door – she had not checked behind the door. Benny whirled round, in time to see the dark silhouette detach itself from the shadows and move towards her. Her whole attention was on the gun in the figure's hand, and through a combination of luck, instinct and raw panic she found herself swinging her rucksack off her shoulder.

The gun came up, and the rucksack connected with it. The figure cried out in pain and surprise as the weapon went spinning away, the rucksack following. The man recovered in an instant and launched himself at Benny, hands tensed in front of him. As his left hand lashed out, he seemed to realise it was Benny and Straklant skidded to a halt just in front of her.

'Oh,' he said. 'It's you.'

'Evidently,' Benny said. 'A word of advice, never raise your hands to a lady.'

'I thought...' He shrugged. 'Well, I don't know...' he admitted.

Across the room, a camera slid forwards into the light, swivelling to stare at them.

'I don't think we should hang around,' Benny said. She grabbed her rucksack while Straklant scooped up his gun. 'I didn't know you had a gun,' she told him. 'I thought you were into old relics and stuff.'

He pulled her into the corridor as the camera rumbled towards them. 'And I thought you were an archaeologist,' he said.

The camera from outside Benny's room was waiting for them. Benny nudged Straklant and pointed to it. Together they ran in the opposite direction.

There was a bend in the corridor, and the two of them slowed as they approached. 'What are they doing?' Straklant asked.

'You don't want to know,' Benny replied as she edged round the corner. 'All clear,' she said as soon as she could see the corridor straighten out again. Straklant was round the corner in a blur, back close to the wall, gun poised. He had obviously done this sort of thing before. Many times before, Benny thought as she watched the gun travel to cover the width of the corridor ahead of them. He held it in both hands, rock steady.

'Let's keep moving,' Straklant said. His voice was low and serious.

'Good plan,' Benny said. She had no idea where they were. The dining room was the other way down the corridor, this way was an unknown. At the end of the corridor was a heavy door. But what lay beyond, neither of them knew. Perhaps they were being driven into a trap. Benny moved forward cautiously after Straklant, trying not to think about the grainy inked images on the monitor. Of Straklant lying in a dark pool.

Several yards along the corridor was an alcove. A holo-image was set in it. The young Munroe Hennessy was at a podium, presumably addressing an unseen gathering. He seemed to be talking to the corridor. His face was set, his hand raised to emphasise whatever point he was making. Behind him and to one side was a camera, capturing the scene. An image captured while the holo-vid was being made.

Despite the circumstances, Benny spared a moment to look at the scene. Certainly Hennessy had cut an impressive figure in his heyday. But that was long ago. Long gone.

She turned and continued down the corridor. Behind her, the camera at the back of the image slid gracefully forwards, slicing through Hennessy and emerging into the pale light of the corridor. Its eye-lens swivelled to follow Benny and Straklant as they reached the door. Then it trundled purposefully after them.

The whole wall was taken up with screens. Dozens of them were arranged in rows in front of the figure hunched over the control panel. Each showed the image relayed from one of the cameras. There were several views of Benny and Straklant. A selection of angles and shots from which to choose. One screen was larger than the others, and central in the wall. A focal point. The master shot.

A thin hand reached out and pressed a control. The image on the main screen switched from a view of Benny and Straklant approaching the door to show the other side of the door. The door swung open and Straklant was through it in a flurry of movement, rolling to one side and coming up into a crouch with the gun ready. It snapped across the corridor ahead, covering every possible angle of attack one after another. Then Straklant got to his feet, Benny appearing behind him.

'Oh he's very good. So very good.'

The image changed again. A long shot of Benny and Straklant making their way along the new section of corridor.

Then a closer shot of Benny, one hand at the strap of her rucksack as she glanced round. 'She's good too. The camera likes her.' A short laugh. 'But not good enough, I'm afraid.'

The hand reached out again. 'Time for our hero to make his move, I think.'

They both turned as the door behind them opened again. Beyond it, further down the corridor they could see two of the cameras gliding slowly forwards. But they were a way back from the door. After a moment, the door closed again. 'What was that for?' Straklant said. 'Just to check we're still here?'

'I don't think so.' Benny pointed along the corridor in front of them. There was another camera waiting in an alcove, its lens just nosing into view as it watched them. She tried to think back to the storyboard. What had happened? Why would a door need to be opened? 'Got it!' She grabbed Straklant's hand and dragged him forwards. 'Come on. Hennessy's after us.'

'What?!'

'Don't you see? They'll add him later. An image. A digital effect. Whatever. But a post-production computer animation can't open a door.'

Straklant slowed. They were almost at the camera. It had emerged fully into the corridor and was waiting for them impassively. 'It can't kill us, either,' he said.

'Maybe not,' Benny said. 'But that's an assumption you can only be wrong about once.'

'Whether I'm right or not,' Straklant replied, 'I think it's time we took the initiative.'

'Oh yes?' They were walking now, catching their breath,

watching the camera ahead of them as it returned their stares. 'What initiative is that then?'

Behind them the door at the end of the corridor swung open again, and two cameras slid through.

'This,' Straklant said as he raised the gun. He aimed it carefully and deliberately at the camera a few yards in front of them. It gave no indication that it was aware of the danger.

The sound was deafening in the corridor, bouncing off the walls and pummelling Benny's ears. The focused blast of compressed energy hit the camera full on and the lens exploded into smithereens. Glass scattered across the floor, crunching under Benny's and Straklant's feet as they moved cautiously forward. The camera had been knocked back by the blast, crashing into the wall. Now it looked misshapen, its main body hanging limply from the central shaft so that it seemed to be looking at its own base.

The camera twitched as Benny edged past it. To the side of the lens she saw for the first time that there was a small hollow tube. Its opening was a dark circle, reminding her of... She frowned. What did it remind her of? She looked at Straklant as he continued down the corridor, his gun still raised, the barrel smoking.

Barrel.

Gun barrel.

'Oh hell,' she said in a low voice. But her words were lost beneath the crashing explosions of sound.

The ground was ripped up at their feet, chips of stone flew from the floor and the wall behind them. The dying camera was knocked off its stand and its two comrades hurtled down the corridor after Benny and Straklant.

'Run!' Benny screamed.

And they ran.

'I can't help feeling this is what they want,' Straklant shouted through the hurricane of noise and flying stonework.

'Maybe,' Benny shouted back. 'Do you want to argue with

them about it?'

They were running faster than the cameras could move. There was another door further along the corridor. The doors off to the side all seemed to be locked and they did not have time to try to break through any of them. Perhaps, Benny thought, they could get through the door then block it behind them. Depending what was waiting on the other side. At least they were far enough ahead now that the shooting had stopped.

'If they do shoot us, won't it spoil their story?' Straklant asked. Benny was glad to hear that he was struggling for breath too.

'It isn't their story I'm worried about actually,' Benny told him. 'And no, I don't think it would. Their hero will just be added holding a big gun.' The cameras were catching up again, and there was an ear-splitting rattle of energy pellets against the corridor walls. 'A very big gun,' Benny screamed through the noise as they quickened their pace.

They crashed through the door, Straklant shouldering it open so hard that it bounced off the wall on the other side and almost hit Benny on the rebound. There was no sign of another camera in front of them. But equally, there was nothing within sight they could use to jam the door shut. The corridor continued ahead.

Benny tried the nearest door. Like all the others they had tried it was locked solid.

'We need a plan,' Straklant said.

'Stay alive,' Benny said. 'That do?'

'Hmm. A bit more strategy. Like find the shuttle.'

They were jogging along the corridor again, waiting for the door behind them to open at any moment. Waiting to break into a run. 'A good secondary objective,' Benny agreed. 'Any suggestions how we do it?'

He somehow managed to shrug while running. 'You?' he asked. 'What do you think we should do?'

'I think we should find the editing suite.'

The door behind them crashed open again. Straklant

swung round and loosed off two shots. The floor just inside the door erupted, and one of the cameras careered off to the side, smashing into the wall and exploding in smoky flames. The corridor was full of smoke, obscuring the other camera.

They both stopped, watching the grey clouds billowing in the confined space. Benny glanced at Straklant. Had he done it? Were they safe now? He returned her glance, and they both grinned. Slowly, hesitantly, they started back down the corridor towards the smoke and the shattered carcass of the camera.

They stopped dead. The second camera emerged unscathed from the smoke, its lens swivelling round as it searched for them – found them. A rattle of gunfire sent shivers of smoke curling away from the gun barrel as the camera headed down the corridor towards them.

The corridor ended in a large conference room. The open space was dominated by a heavy glass-topped table. High-backed chairs were arranged round it. At one end of the room was a holo-projection screen. It was blank. There were several doorways – open doorways – off the room.

'So what's this editing suite thing?' Straklant asked.

'I don't really know. But I guess it's where he controls the cameras from,' Benny said.

As if responding to her words, three cameras slid forwards from alcoves round the room. A fourth emerged at speed from beside the doorway where they had entered, barrelling into Straklant's back and sending him flying. He fell forwards into the side of the table, his gun knocked from his grip and skidding across the glass surface. He scrabbled to retrieve it, but it was just out of reach.

Benny turned at once, swinging her rucksack in a low arc, round and up. It caught the camera under the lens just as its gun went off. The main part of the camera was knocked upwards, the energy pellets peppering the ceiling. Plaster and woodwork exploded and fell. Benny dived out of the way, swinging her rucksack again, this time sliding it across the table top.

The rucksack caught Straklant's gun and sent it spinning back towards him. He grabbed it, turned, aimed and fired in one motion. The camera, still swivelling and dipping as it tried to get focused, exploded in flames.

'You keep them busy,' Benny called. She had to shout above the sound of gunfire from the other cameras. 'I'll try to find this editing suite and stop him.'

Straklant did not reply. He nodded once to show he had heard. But he was already running across the room, avoiding the gunfire, firing off blasts of energy whenever he got the chance. Most of them went wide. But he was drawing the cameras' fire.

Benny hesitated only an instant. Then she dived under the table and started to crawl across the floor towards an unguarded doorway. She wasn't sure, but the corridor beyond looked better lit, better furnished. As if it led into the main part of the building. The others were stark and drab and dim. Unused.

She thought – she hoped – that they had not seen her. The table top was glass, tinted but still transparent. She had to be quick. While they were distracted by Straklant. She glanced round, wondering briefly if she could get out of the doorway they had come in, and back to the part of the house she knew. But the camera that had been chasing them appeared in the opening. Its lens-eye swung back and forth, as if searching. It seemed uninterested in Straklant, who was sheltering behind one of the chairs as he snapped in a fresh energy cartridge. The back of the chair was disintegrating under a storm of gunfire. But he was concentrating on the job, totally focused, totally professional.

Benny looked from Straklant back towards the camera. Just as it looked towards her. For a moment, they both stared at each other. Then Benny tightened her grip on the strap of her rucksack and crawled as fast as she could towards the opposite side of the room.

The sound of shattering glass was even louder than the rattle of gunfire. The table above her exploded into fragments, sharp flying fragments. They rained down on Benny's back, cut into her face, lodged in her hair, sprinkled across her rucksack. She screamed in surprise and pain. It took her a second to realise she was still crawling, even though the table above was gone. The gunfire ripped into the floor between her legs and she leaped up and ran.

As soon as she had time to think logically, as soon as she was clear of the cameras, Benny came to the conclusion that the editing suite must be close to the dining room. Keeping her fingers carefully crossed, she decided that the main living area must be fairly compact. Hennessy obviously did not find it easy to get around in his chair. It seemed sensible then to keep the rooms he used most in the same area of the house. The guest rooms had been off in a wing – the wing that Benny and Straklant had run the length of to escape the cameras. But the dining room, and the main living area would be a hub, a central zone. Compact and together.

Probably.

Trying not to think about what to do if she was wrong and how long it would take to search the entire house while avoiding the cameras, Benny managed to double back to the dining room and start her search from there. She moved slowly, cautiously, hugging the shadows and hoping that Straklant was all right.

She knew she had found it as soon as she opened the door. The whole of the wall opposite the door was covered in screens. Most of them showed views of Straklant. He seemed to be having a running battle with several cameras in what looked like a storage area. Racks of shelving were overturned, preventing the free movement of the cameras. Straklant was pinned down behind another set of shelves. As Benny watched, a collection of books and holo-spheres was pushed off a shelf, and Straklant's gun appeared in the resulting gap. There was a soundless burst of fire from the end of the gun before it withdrew. One of the screens went blank, and Benny resisted the urge to cheer.

Partly this was because she had caught sight of the image on another screen. It showed the conference room. The main point of focus was the shattered remains of the conference table. And lying face down amongst the debris, on a sea of broken glass, was Benny herself. Her face was twisted to one side, the visible eye closed. She was dressed in only a t-shirt.

'You died under the table, I'm afraid.'

The voice was low, measured and without a trace of regret. Benny swung round, to see that the door had closed behind her.

'We shall have to change the clothing to match. Matte in the rucksack, of course. Actually, that's a still image of you asleep on the bed. You look so peaceful. But in fact, you fidget a lot you know, kick off the covers.' Fedora Bronsan smiled thinly, her lips stretching back over her teeth. 'It's interesting to watch.' She was holding a gun.

'I bet it is.' Benny took a step backwards. 'You like to watch, don't you.' She kept her own attention on the gun. 'I bet your friend Hennessy gets a kick out of it too.'

Bronsan sighed. 'I'm afraid dear Munroe gets a kick, as you say, out of nothing these days.' She leaned past Benny, uncomfortably close for a moment, as she pressed a button and the picture on one of the screens changed. Now it showed a bedroom. The figure lying asleep was Hennessy. Beside him, an assortment of tubes and wires ran from the bed to a box on the bedside cabinet. A box that flashed with lights, which displayed a heart-beat blip peaking on a graph. At the top of the box a diaphragm inflated and deflated slowly, almost in time to the beating of the heart.

'He can't even breath on his own when he's asleep,' Bronsan said. There was genuine sadness in her voice.

'I doubt he'll be making much of a comeback then,' Benny said. Still she watched the gun, but it was held firm and unwavering.

'Oh yes he will!' Bronsan said with sudden anger. The gun came up, and she whipped it across Benny's face.

Benny fell away with a cry, falling to the floor, her hand out behind her to break the fall.

Bronsan stepped forwards, towering over her. 'His screen presence, his image, was always more compelling, more attractive than he was himself. He'll make a comeback all right.'

On the screens, Straklant dived across the room, coming up and firing in a single fluid movement before diving for more cover as the cameras shot back.

'Oh this is better than I ever could have hoped,' Bronsan said as she watched. 'Munroe Hennessy will once again capture the hearts and minds and love of the galaxy. And just think, you'll be playing a starring role alongside him.'

'Oh really?' Benny made no attempt to get up. 'I'm thinking. And I'd have thought that was your privilege. Isn't your place at his side?'

'I believed so once.' There was a dreamy, wistful quality in her voice. 'But I was wrong.' Her voice hardened again. 'No, my place is in control.' She seemed to savour the word.

Another screen blanked out. 'You don't seem very in control to me,' Benny said quietly. Her arm was still behind her, still supporting her body. But her hand was holding a cable. A big, thick, chunky, rubberised cable. She had no idea what it was, but she reckoned it was large enough to be important.

Bronsan spared a glance at the screens. As she did so, several more of the pictures vanished into blackness. 'No!' she said in surprise. 'That's the other side of the house, how can that be?' She stared a moment longer.

Benny braced herself, holding the cable tight.

Bronsan turned back to Benny. 'What are you doing?' she demanded. 'Who is helping you?'

'Wouldn't you like to know?' Benny said brightly. Maybe there was a technical problem of some sort. Or maybe Straklant had done something clever to the systems. Perhaps he had found the equivalent of the fuse box and was tripping switches.

Several more monitors blanked out. And Bronsan turned back to them, the gun still pointed at Benny. 'Stop this!' she shouted. 'Stop it now, or I'll blow off your leg.'

'Blow off yourself,' Benny shot back as she moved. She rolled to one side, dragging the cable with her. It tore free from its socket in the wall with a shower of sparks.

The screens all went black. Sparks erupted from the end of the cable. Bronsan screamed with anger and surprise. And fired the gun.

The shot went wide as Benny was still rolling. She struggled to her feet as Bronsan swung round, bringing the gun up again. Due to luck as much as planning, the end of the cable connected with Bronsan as Benny struggled to move away from the gun.

For a second, the woman was bathed in blue light that shimmered and rippled round her body. She screamed, dropping the gun. Then the cable bucked in Benny's hands as if it were alive, and she pushed it away from her, leaving it to writhe on the floor. Fedora Bronsan crumpled and fell. She spasmed and convulsed on the floor, curling into a foetal position and moaning quietly.

'You should get a stunt double,' Benny said as she stepped over the unconscious woman.

The cameras too were unconscious. Benny passed several as she sought out Straklant. One was lying on its side, the lens cracked across. Another was skewed into a wall, its 'eye' angled downwards in a sad, almost baleful manner. It seemed odd to Benny that they were all connected into the same circuit as the screens. Perhaps Straklant had managed to knock them out somehow? But she had to admit to herself that it seemed unlikely.

She found him emerging from the storage area, and he confirmed her suspicions.

'They didn't all stop at once,' he said. 'I thought it was something you'd done. One after another they just sort of ground to a halt.'

Benny shook her head. 'I don't think it was me.' She felt cold suddenly. The elation had died away. 'Let's find Hennessy.'

'But wasn't he –'

'No,' she told him. 'That was Fedora Bronsan.'

'So maybe it was Hennessy that turned off the cameras.' They were making their way carefully back towards the main part of the house.

'No it wasn't. He's sleeping peacefully.'

The figure stepped out of a doorway in front of them. Every part of the figure was covered, so it was impossible to tell if it was male, female, or even human. It was wearing a black one-piece assault suit, the face hidden by a blast helmet, the visor lowered. The voice was filtered through the helmet, distorted and impersonal. 'I had to disconnect the control circuits to disable the alarm system.' The figure started walking towards them. 'And to make sure I could get in safely.'

'Why?' Straklant asked, pushing Benny back behind him.

The figure was moving easily, almost like a cat – ease and threat intermingled. At its side, the figure was holding a handblaster. Like everything else about it, the grip seemed normal, relaxed. Dangerously relaxed. 'So I could kill you,' the distorted voice said. And the gun came up.

Straklant reacted first, pushing Benny one way as he dived the other. The space in between them exploded into vivid orange and Benny felt the heat of the energy wave as she was thrown further across the corridor. Then she was up, running after Straklant who was already ahead of her. He ducked as another wave of energy spouted over his head and burned across the wall.

'It's all go, isn't it?!' Benny yelled as they rounded a corner. She overtook Straklant, pleased at his expression of surprise and annoyance. 'This way!'

Benny led him back through the house, doubling round to try to get to where she thought Hennessy's bedroom must be. They seemed to have thrown off the faceless assassin. For the moment.

'Whoever it is, they know we have to get back to the shuttle,' Straklant pointed out.

'Mmm. But who is it?' Benny wondered. 'A chum of Dale Pettit's?'

'Who?'

'You know, the guy who was after the Doomsday Manuscript back at Braxiatel's. The guy you killed.'

'Oh. Him.'

'He must have been working for someone. Someone who wants the thing as much as we do.' Benny stopped outside a door. There was a large gold star on it. Beside the door a camera stood on guard, its body angled downwards deferentially. 'I think we're here,' she said, and pushed the door open.

Beside her, Straklant gave the camera an experimental shove. It was extremely heavy, and rolled only a few inches before it slowed and stopped. The lens did not move or react. Completely inert.

'Just checking,' he said, and followed her through the door.

The whole room was breathing. The beeping from the heart monitor seemed to punctuate the rasp of the oxygen pump that forced air into the sleeping man's lungs. The lighting was a subdued shade of blue. Hennessy seemed even older and smaller laid out on the bed. His eyes were closed, his chest rising and falling in time to the breathing of the pump.

Benny touched him lightly on the shoulder, and immediately his eyes flickered open. Surprise registered on his face as he moved slightly, trying to see who she was as she leaned over him.

'What do you want?' he croaked. His voice was barely audible without the enhancement. 'Is it time to get up? Where's Miss Bronsan?'

'She's having a little rest,' Benny told him.

'And what we want is the Doomsday Manuscript,' Straklant said bluntly.

Hennessy looked puzzled.

'I'm afraid we lied to you,' Benny said. She took a deep breath. 'I'm sorry.'

'Lied?' He twisted slightly in the bed. There was a tube running out of the side of his mouth, Benny could see now as he shifted position. 'Lied to me?'

'We're not from a studio,' she said. 'We don't have a script.' His expression was unreadable. 'I'm sorry,' she said again.

His face twisted, his lips curling back and a high-pitched shriek emerged from between his bloodless lips. At first Benny thought he was crying. His eyes were moist and his body contorted with effort. Then as his expression softened, she realised he was laughing. It was so bizarre that she almost laughed as well.

'I know that,' he said when he could get the machine's breath back. 'What studio would want me?' His head moved slightly so he could look down at his wasted body. 'In this condition?' He laughed again. 'My day is over,' he said. 'Long over.' There was a trace of sadness in his voice, of regret. But no more than that.

'You know?' Benny breathed.

'It's pretty obvious,' he rasped back. 'It's only Fedora who can't see it. I play along, I try to maintain the pretence.' He craned to see Benny properly. 'Between you and me,' he wheezed, 'I think she's gone a bit crazy. But I would never dare tell her.' He settled back into the pillow. 'She has a temper, that one. Otherwise I'd have sacked her long ago.'

'Sack her,' Benny advised. 'And you're certainly right about the crazy thing.'

'It's in the library,' he said as if in reply. 'On the shelf with the ells.'

'What is?' Straklant demanded shortly. Benny glared at him.

'The Doomsday Manuscript,' Hennessy said with an effort. 'Half of it, anyway. It's fascinating, you know. Load of bollocks of course,' he added with a wheeze. 'But a damned fine read.'

'Thank you.' Benny tried to shoo Straklant away from the bed, but he was crowding closer. She gave up and turned back to Hennessy. 'Just one thing,' she said.

His eyes were closing as she spoke. They hesitated, half open and half shut. 'Yes?'

'What are ells?'

'Ells, what do you mean?'

'You said it's on the shelf with the ells,' Straklant reminded him.

Hennessy gave a wheezing laugh and his eyes closed. 'The letter "L",' he said. 'For Lacey.' In a moment he seemed to be asleep.

Benny watched him, checked that his breathing was again regular, then pushed past Straklant and made for the door.

'I don't think we should hang around,' she called back to him. 'L for leather might be more appropriate.'

Straklant waited until she was out of the room. Then he walked round to the back of the life-support systems. There was a single power cable socketed into the back of the unit. He glanced up to check that Benny was still out of sight, then pulled the cable free and dropped it to the floor.

The beep of the heart monitor stopped at once. The artifical lung deflated, and remained still. The noise in the room died.

Straklant patted Hennessy's shoulder as he eased past him again. 'Sweet dreams,' he murmured, and left the room.

Benny was standing just outside the door. But she wasn't waiting for him. Just in front of her, Fedora Bronsan was standing shakily, holding a gun.

'What have you been saying to him?' Bronsan demanded. Her voice was as shaky as the gun which wavered and quivered, but never enough to leave Benny safe from a shot if it came.

Straklant could not tell if she had seen him. But he had to assume that she had, so he kept coming out of the room rather than try to duck back inside. The last thing he wanted was anyone to come back into the room.

'We didn't have to tell him anything,' Benny said. 'He knows you're quite mad. Crazy, I think he said.'

'Crazy,' Straklant agreed. He smiled at Bronsan and leaned against the camera that stood just outside the door. He felt it shift slightly as he applied some of his weight to it.

'You're lying,' the woman shrieked through gritted teeth. Her eyes were blazing, the gun steadier as she jabbed it towards Benny.

'And I'm sure there was something else,' Benny said, tapping her teeth thoughtfully. 'Oh yes, that was it.' She snapped her fingers as if conjuring the memory out of the air. 'You're fired.'

'What?' Bronsan screamed. Her whole attention was on Benny now. Her knuckles whitened as she applied pressure to the trigger mechanism.

At the same moment, Straklant applied his full weight and strength to the camera. He braced himself against the doorframe as he heaved it towards her.

It was almost soundless as it slid forwards, gliding over the smooth floor, gathering speed. The heavy camera caught Fedora Bronsan as she fired. The energy bolt slammed into the side of the camera housing. Benny dived away. Straklant watched in satisfaction as the camera kept rolling forwards. Bronsan's arms were thrown up as she collapsed under its weight, pushed backwards into the wall of the corridor. There was a crunching sound, a half cry of pain and surprise, and the camera came to rest.

A hand flopped out under the legs of the camera. Pale and white. And after it, the dark blood trickled round the castors.

'Which way is the library, do you suppose?' Straklant asked. He licked his lips.

Straklant watched the door while Benny checked the shelves. It wasn't hard to find the manuscript – a single holosphere correctly filed under Lacey. Everything seemed to be filed by author, so this made perfect sense.

Too nervous and cautious to be elated, Benny led the way back to the shuttle. All the way they kept a wary lookout for the suited figure that had tried to kill them. But they reached the shuttle without incident.

Straklant insisted on checking the engines and looking all round for booby traps or tracers. But he found nothing. They strapped themselves in for launch, Benny nursing the manuscript, her rucksack stowed in a locker. She held her breath as Straklant initiated the launch sequence. In a few seconds they would either be rising from the pad and heading out into space, flying towards Kasagrad and the Lost Tomb of Rablev. Or they would be dead, flying round space in little pieces.

Only when they were breaking out of the gravity field did Benny allow herself to relax. 'Not as clever as we thought he might be,' she observed.

Straklant grinned back. 'Maybe he had other things to do.'

Benny laughed. 'Like looking for this you mean?' She held up the manuscript. 'I wonder who he is,' she said, almost to herself. 'And what he's up to now.'

Hennessy's breathing was erratic, ragged, struggling. He twisted and turned helplessly on the bed, gasping for air. His eyes were open, bulging wide.

The dark-suited figure spared him only the briefest glance as it entered the room. Then at once it went to the life-support system and examined it. After a moment it found the power cable lying disconnected on the floor.

The respirator started immediately the power was reconnected. The heart beep was fast and irregular. It began to settle into a more gentle rhythm almost at once. Hennessy's face was wet with perspiration, but his breathing was easier now. Before long he was able to gasp out a few words:

'Who are you?'

The figure standing by the bed reached over to wipe the sweat from his face, dabbing at his forehead with a hand towel from the side of the unit. Then it straightened up, and took off the helmet.

Hennessy's face was a mask of surprise.

6
Space Run

It did not take them long to realise they had a problem. They were barely clear of orbit when the aft scanners told them there had been another launch. Someone was following them – in a bigger, faster, and better-armed ship than theirs.

'How do we know it's better armed?' Benny had asked, looking dubiously at the blip of light on the scanner.

'Because we aren't armed at all,' Straklant told her.

'Fair enough.'

The small shuttle rolled sideways, alarms going off and warning lights flashing before Benny could ask how they could be sure that the pursuing ship was armed. She was thrown back in her chair as Straklant struggled with the controls, trying to coax more power from the engines.

'Can we outrun it?' Benny shouted above the alarms.

'I don't know. Yet,' he shouted back.

The ship rocked again under another near-impact. 'At least they're not getting any closer,' Straklant said as the alarms settled down into a steady ear-splitting tone.

'Do they need to?'

'I'm not sure,' he admitted. 'They could have knocked us out of space easily by now. If they wanted to.'

'They don't want to,' Benny said.

'Certainly seems that way.' He was hunched over the control console, concentrating on keeping the ship from rolling.

'I'm sure of it,' Benny said. She held up the holosphere they had taken from Hennessy's library. 'They're after this. They know we have it, and they want it – intact, not in little bits.'

The ship rolled again, a ball of fire blotting out the forward scanner for several seconds before they emerged, pitching and yawing into the darkness of space again.

'You're sure about that, are you?' Straklant said.

'Not entirely,' Benny said. 'Maybe they're trying to slow us down. Knock out the engines or something. How far is it to Kasagrad? Will we make it?'

'Not far. A couple of hours to the exclusion zone.' He turned to her for a moment as the ship levelled out again. 'And I have no idea if we'll make it. We just have to hope we run into some Axis shipping before then. Someone who can help.'

'I'm not sure I care for the way you said "run into",' Benny told him. 'And what do you mean, "exclusion zone"?'

The way Straklant explained it and the way that Benny understood it were not entirely the same. His explanation was that the good people and government of neutral Kasagrad were pleased and happy that the forces of the Fifth Axis were there to keep unwanted attention away from their home and regulate the incoming and outgoing trade.

When Benny put this information together with what she already knew of the situation, she reached a rather different conclusion. Kasagrad was a strategic embarrassment to the Fifth Axis. It was a supposedly neutral planet within their assimilated territories – a planet they did not totally and directly control that was behind their front line. They couldn't take it easily because of the sophisticated defence grid that surrounded the planet. And they couldn't just take out the grid as the control centre was an apparently impregnable fortress citadel built during the Time of the Tombs. Their only military option was a direct attack – which would cost time, money and massive loss of life on both sides.

So, Braxiatel had explained to Benny before she left with Straklant, the Fifth Axis was playing a different game – a political and economic one. By controlling the trade in and out of the planet, they were slowly but surely tightening a noose round the collective neck of the Kasagrad government. Resist, and they'd lose all outside contact – in effect they'd be under siege. But co-operate and the food and other supplies would be allowed through the cordon.

'It's a common enough technique,' he had said. 'Pretty blunt, but effective. There are a dozen smaller powers trying the same things at various points in this part of space from the Dendronian sanctions against the Grombi to the Federation blockade of Venedel because they want to cede.'

He had seemed set to enumerate each and every situation, so Benny had gently prompted him: 'Okay,' she said. 'I think we understand the what. Can we discuss the why and wherefore a little now?'

The eventual goal, it wasn't actually hard to deduce, was a Kasagrad government that acceded to the will of the Fifth Axis so completely that the planet was effectively assimilated into the Territories.

But all that would take time. And if the Fifth Axis saw a more direct route to its objective, there was no doubt in Benny's mind that it would take it.

The effect on the populace of the planet itself she could only guess at. But there would be factions for and against resisting the Fifth Axis; there would be blackmarketeers capitalising on the lack of supplies; there would be informers and agents and sympathisers for every faction... Actually, Benny was looking forward to arriving on Kasagrad and getting involved in it all.

Not least, she decided as another wave of energy blasted the shuttle sideways and rolled it over on its back, because that would mean she had escaped from this mess.

They were so nearly there. It had been a hectic journey. Benny's intention, once she realised that if she was about to die there wasn't a thing she could do about it, was to examine Lacey's half of the Doomsday Manuscript. But Straklant was reluctant to let her switch her attention from helping him watch the scanners and instruments. It did not seem to Benny that she was helping a whole lot, but if it gave him the added confidence he needed to keep them alive, then it was the least she could do.

So the holosphere remained unread. She jammed it between her rucksack and a bulkhead for whatever protection she could. Luckily, she told herself, the things were pretty much indestructible. That was the great thing about using holo-imaging. Like a hologram, if you broke it into pieces, each piece still contained the entirety of the data. The quality, the resolution dropped, just as a fragment of a hologram shows a dimmer but identical image. But the data would still be there, recoverable.

They were so nearly there when the engines cut out. Straklant had been rolling and spinning the shuttle the whole way so as to present a less easy target to the ship behind. Occasionally the pursuit ship managed to get closer; sometimes they managed to pull clear. But for the most part they ran and the ship following them spat fire and tried to keep up. Then a single, well-placed blast caught the control linkage to the engines.

The sound of the motors was replaced by the insistent buzz of the alarm that told them what had happened. Straklant swore. He punched at the controls for a few seconds, then gave up and raised his hands in the air in an expression of helplessness. 'We're almost in sight of the blockade fleet,' he complained, forgetting for the moment that the term he had used before was 'regulatory authorities.'

Well, if nothing else, Benny thought at least he wasn't so stupid as to believe the rubbish he'd told her earlier. But any further thoughts were distracted by the hissing sound of inert gas being released under pressure and the accompanying siren that warned of a fire.

'The electrics have ignited,' Straklant said. Already they could taste the gas, smell the smoke. 'Better suit up.'

There were pressurised survival suits hanging on a rack behind the forward bulkhead. They struggled into them, pulling them over their clothes. The smoke was getting thicker, clawing at the back of Benny's throat as she fought to snap the helmet clips shut, the heavy gloves scrabbling to gain a purchase. Once they were closed, the suit would pump away the impurities trapped in the helmet with her. But not until. She coughed, doubling up with the effort, managing to click the last catch as she did so.

Straklant's voice was filtered through the helmet radio circuits. 'The control systems will deal with the fire. But we can't stop them docking.'

'Whoever they are,' Benny said, partly to check her own radio was working. She was breathing heavily. Her throat was clogged with smoke and gas.

They made their way back to the cabin. 'What are our options?' Benny asked as Straklant checked over the controls.

'Limited,' he said. 'By that.' He jabbed a gauntleted hand towards the scanners. 'The ship that was chasing us is closing in, extending a docking tube. And there's another ship coming in fast.'

'Same sort?'

'Bigger. Much bigger.'

Benny pondered this. 'And the chances are that these are friends of the ship that's docking.'

The ship rocked slightly under their feet and a loud clang rang out, clearly audible through the helmet. Benny and Straklant exchanged looks through their misty face plates. The smoke was clearing, and they both then turned to look towards the back of the ship. Towards the airlock.

'Escape pods?' Benny suggested.

Straklant grabbed the rucksack on the way. He scooped up the holosphere they had taken from Hennessy's library and stuffed it inside. 'You first,' he said as he swung open the door to the escape pod section. 'Look after the sphere.'

There were two pods. Straklant hustled Benny into the first, then handed her the rucksack. He stepped back from the door and it clanged shut.

At once Benny was back at the door. 'Hey,' she shouted into her radio. 'Where are you going?'

113

'The other pod. No point in giving them one easy target.'
Straklant's voice was already fading. The radio link was
intended only for use within the ship, within very close
proximity.

'No, you're right,' Benny said glumly as she strapped
herself in and hugged her rucksack to her chest. 'Let's give
them two easy targets.' She reached out for the launch lever,
grabbed the heavy metal bar with her gloved hand. And
paused. 'Unless...'

From further down the ship came a rumble of sound. The
floor vibrated, and Benny twisted to see through the small
porthole window beside her. The stubby cylindrical shape of
the second pod flashed past, twisting slightly about its axis
as it went.

'Straklant?' she called. 'Straklant!' But there was no reply.
Out of range.

Benny twisted further. She could just see the pursuit ship,
attached to the shuttle by a short tube. Straklant's pod had
skimmed dangerously close to the ship as it passed. Beyond
it, gleaming in the starlight, was another ship – much larger.
A cruiser, its missile tubes and gun turrets plainly visible as it
eased through space.

'Escape pod launch sequence activated. Launch in twenty
seconds... Nineteen... Eighteen...'

Benny slammed the door shut and locked it, cutting off
the sound of the voice. 'You'd better be right about this,' she
murmured, pulling on her rucksack. It was difficult to get it
over the bulky spacesuit, but she did not have time to adjust
the straps. A few more seconds, that was all. Too late to
change her mind now.

She was standing beside the pod, in the space between
the pod and the wall of the small hanger which housed it.
Behind the pod was the airlock that any second now would
open, and the pod would be heaved hydraulically into space,
its motors cutting in only when it was safely clear of the ship.
Benny braced herself against the hull of the pod, holding on

as best she could to the railings that formed a maintenance ladder running up and over a bulkhead.

'This is a simple plan,' she told herself. 'Simple, but crazy.'

The airlock door shuddered open and Benny held tight to avoid being sucked out with the evaporating air. Then the pod was moving, silently thrown into the airless vacuum. She struggled to stay attached to the side, fought to keep her grip as the pod passed through the airlock door. Then she was spinning with it, disoriented and alone. She caught fleeting, passing glimpses of the three spaceships, desperately tried to keep her bearings and work out where she was in relation to the ship that had pursued them. They would pass close to it. Wouldn't they? Straklant had.

But what if the pods were launched in different directions. Actually, a calm, inner voice told her, that would make sense – that would mean they avoided colliding. 'Shut up,' she told herself through gritted teeth. And she breathed a heavy, audible sigh of relief as the docking tube passed over the top of the pod and she caught sight of the pursuit ship looming massively above her.

And she let go of the pod.

She was spinning helplessly, not far from the ship. But her momentum meant she was moving away from it. No problem, she told herself, no problem. She fumbled at the backpack, feeling round her rucksack to try to find the air intake – the tube that carried the air into her suit. This was the easy bit, she told herself. Just hold your breath, disconnect the pipe and use the escaping, pressurised air to push you over to the pursuit ship. You can do it. You can. All you need is...

Then realisation dawned. As the ship spun under her feet again, smaller this time than last, she realised that the suit was a completely sealed unit. There was no pipe. The whole system was contained inside the suit. The only way to get at it was to rip the thing open – and let in the vacuum. She was drifting away from the ship, alone and with a limited supply of air.

She looked all round, and saw the pod twisting away from her. She was staring up at the bottom of it. There was a flicker of light from the base of the cylinder and she realised something else. The engines were about to ignite. And she was right behind them.

Benny experienced a moment of absolute calm as she knew there was nothing she could do. She watched, detached, as the engines flared into life. Only when the blast of energy caught her and sent her flying backwards did she react.

She laughed.

It was a painful experience – she was hot, buffeted and bruised as her body was flung through space. But she laughed anyway – with relief and at the irony of it. Her back slammed into the hull of the pursuit ship and she twisted round, scrabbling for a hold, still laughing. The heat of the engines had abated as the pod flew ever faster away from her, in the direction of the approaching cruiser. Benny spared it a glance, saw the grappling hooks snaking out from the huge ship to snare it, then started to climb over the hull towards the secondary hatch.

Only when she reached the hatch did Benny look again at the cruiser. She could see her own escape pod being dragged into a docking bay. Beyond the cruiser, another pod emerged from its shadow, drifting into sight. Straklant. The pod spun lazily in the light of the stars, receding slowly from the cruiser and heading towards the rim of the planet in the distance. Just as Benny was about to look away, just as she was about to turn her attention back to the hatch and the opening mechanism, a beam of light lanced out from the cruiser. It stabbed through the darkness of space, searching out the distant pod. For a moment the intense light played across the metal surface.

Then the fragile escape pod exploded in a soundless maelstrom of orange and red and yellow. Debris spun outwards from the blast. The light faded. Benny caught her breath and looked away.

The ship was empty. Although it was larger than the shuttle, it looked as though it was designed for a crew of just one person. Benny let herself in through the airlock, and closed it behind her. She made her way carefully along towards the flight deck, tip-toeing past the open hatch that led into the docking tube.

She spared a glance down the tube, and saw a suited figure close to the far end. The same person, she was pretty sure, as had tried to kill them at Hennessy's. The figure moved with the same easy and assured gait.

Benny had almost reached the flight deck when the klaxon went off. She thought at first that it was an anti-intruder alarm. But as she hurried towards the pilot's chair, she could hear the feminine voice of the flight computer announcing calmly: 'Incoming... Incoming... Incoming...'

'Incoming what?' Benny wondered out loud. But she knew as soon as she checked the forward screen. It showed an image of the battle cruiser, showed it turning slowly and ponderously towards the pursuit ship. Showed a bolt of lightning searing out towards the screen. 'What the hell is that?' she said, but she already knew.

Her radio link was on the same frequency as the flight computer. It paused in its litany of 'incoming' to remark: 'Ship identified as Battle Cruiser Potemkin, currently serving with the Fifth Axis Northern Fleet.'

Then the energy bolt hit, and Benny was knocked from the chair. The voice of the computer was drowned by the sound of the sirens and alarms. Smoke started to pour from the sides of the cabin, and instinctively Benny backed away. She had to get out of here, that much was obvious. Or rather, she decided, she had to get this ship out of here.

It was still bucking and rolling from the impact and resulting damage as she staggered back towards the main hatch. She had to get it closed before she could move the ship – not just to keep the air in, but to keep anyone else out. Sure enough, the suited figure she had seen in the docking tube was making its way swiftly back towards the ship, probably with the same thoughts of flight rather than fight.

The hatch was heavy – achingly heavy. Benny had to strain to shift it. It was easier once it was moving, but as she swung it slowly shut, Benny could be seen from the tube. And she could see down it too – could see the figure returning to the ship as it paused, as it saw her, as it started to run. The motion was slowed by the lack of gravity, a pushing, floating motion as the figure increased speed.

And still the hatchway was closing too slowly. The figure would get to the hatch before Benny could close it.

The radio crackled in Benny's helmet. 'There you are,' a distorted, static-ridden voice exclaimed. 'I've been looking for you.'

'That's nice,' Benny forced out as she shoved the door harder. It moved slightly quicker for a moment. Then stopped.

The suited figure was jammed in the door, pushing it back towards Benny, forcing it open. Benny could see the blaster holstered at the figure's side, could see a hand moving slowly towards it as the figure braced the door open with its body.

So Benny let go of the hatchway door. It swung suddenly back towards her, but she was expecting it and stood aside. The figure on the other side of the door was not expecting it though, and stumbled forwards off balance.

Benny leaned back against the side wall of the airlock entrance and kicked out as hard as she could. Her foot caught the figure in the chest, knocking it backwards as it stumbled. With a crackling, incomprehensible cry the figure fell back through the hatchway and tumbled several yards down the tube. Exhilarated, adrenalin pumping, Benny forced the hatchway closed.

The dark-helmeted face appeared at the hatch porthole a few seconds later. A hand came up and scrabbled at the glass. Benny took a step backwards. She smiled, though she doubted that the figure could see that. And she waved, a cheery happy bye-bye-thanks-for-coming wave.

The figure paused, confused. Then it seemed to realise what Benny was about to do, turned away from the hatch and started running for the other end of the tube.

Benny watched through the thick, distorting glass of the window. 'Good luck, mate,' she said without feeling. Then, without another thought for whoever it was, she ran to the flight deck.

The fire had subsided somewhat and the alarms were less strident. But the cruiser was looming threateningly on the screen and the computer was calmly intoning: 'Incoming...' again, over and over.

Somehow, Benny got the ship moving. It turned slowly, so slowly, and the next energy wave caught the side of it, throwing her across the flight deck again. But the integrity of the hull seemed undiminished. Somehow she managed to steer it away from the cruiser, to pick up a degree of speed. She had no doubt that the bigger ship could catch her if it wanted, but a final lance of energy had set fire to the interior and probably they knew the ship was dying.

She saw the shuttle motionless in space, the docking tube hanging limply from its main hatch. A third escape pod was twisting silently away from it. The suited figure – the person who was trying to kill her – had also escaped it seemed.

As far as Benny could tell, the cruiser gave up following as soon as it was apparent that there was no way the ship could survive. Benny had it diving headlong into the exclusion zone, through the mine field, towards Kasagrad.

'There had better be an escape pod that's capable of re-entry,' Benny said as she set the autopilot and headed back down the ship. Her rucksack was lying where she had left it by the secondary hatch. She grabbed it and found the evacuation bay.

Only when she was in the pod, only when she was away from the crippled, flaming craft, only when she was slicing down through the atmosphere of the planet getting uncomfortably hotter by the moment did she spare a moment to open the rucksack and check the contents.

Only then did she find that the holosphere containing Lacey's half of the manuscript – the holosphere she had been searching for and which Straklant had given his life for – was not there. She looked up at the ceiling of the pod. Somewhere above her, probably engulfed in a burning spaceship or the fragments of an escape pod, was the final part of the answer to the riddle of the Lost Tomb of Rablev.

Her last thought as the pod impacted with the ground and she was flung violently against the harness, her last thought as her vision swam and she lost consciousness, was that nobody would ever solve that riddle.

Interlude II

The call came through just as Braxiatel was leaving.

He returned to his desk, a trace of impatience in his voice as he keyed the console. 'Yes?'

'Call from the residence of Dr Josiah Vanderbilt,' the AI whispered soothingly, well aware that it was the middle of the night and unwilling to disturb anyone.

Braxiatel settled himself back at his desk. 'Put him on,' he said, angling himself so he could see the screen set into the top of his desk.

It turned out to be a her not a him. The head and shoulders of a middle-aged woman appeared. There were dark rings under her eyes that almost matched the sombre material of the jacket she was wearing.

'Irving Braxiatel?' she asked, her voice efficient and clipped.

'Yes.'

'I understand you have been trying to contact Dr Vanderbilt.'

'Indeed,' he told her. 'He hasn't replied to an invitation I sent him. I didn't really expect him to, of course, but it seemed courteous to call. And I wanted to ask him something.'

She attempted to smile. 'That was kind.'

There was an awkward pause, and then Braxiatel asked: 'I'm sorry, but you are...?'

'Mona Wyrd. I was Dr Vanderbilt's secretary.' Her eyes widened slightly as she spoke.

As if, Braxiatel thought, she was trying to tell him something, but didn't want to say it outright. 'I assume,' he said slowly, 'given that the doctor has not returned my calls himself, that your use of the past tense is significant?'

She blinked, then sniffed. 'Yes.' The word was a gasp. She wiped an eye with the back of her hand, murmuring: 'I'm sorry.'

Braxiatel was not someone who found sympathy easy to offer. Especially over a remote link. But he was astute enough to know that, and didn't try. 'He was an old man,' he said gently. 'I'm saddened by the news, but I can't say I'm surprised.'

She looked back at him, eyes still moist. When she spoke, her voice had regained a little of its earlier composure. 'If he had died in his sleep, simply slipped away, I would agree with you. We all expected it, as you did. Sooner rather than later. But...' Her voice tailed off and she bit her lip as her face crumpled.

'But?' With a feeling of deep apprehension, Braxiatel leaned forwards. 'Tell me what happened.'

It took her a while, but eventually she was able to recount how she had found the body. How the tall, thin man had shown himself out. How she had taken lunch through to Dr Vanderbilt who had so much work to finish up. How she had found him slumped over his desk, a neat hole drilled through the centre of his left eye.

'I'm sorry we didn't inform you when we sent out the funeral notices,' she said through her dying tears. 'It was difficult to contact all his colleagues, and I'm afraid the invitation you mentioned was not amongst Dr Vanderbilt's belongings.'

'No,' said Braxiatel softly. 'No, I don't suppose it was.'

He sat at his desk in the muted light for a long time after she had broken the connection. The only movement in the room was that of his fingertips tapping gently together in time with the ticking of the clock.

The fact that Vanderbilt was dead meant that they were serious. It also meant that whatever they were up to was not expected to take long. They would know that the death would soon be common knowledge, and the fact that there was not even the pretence of an accident about it suggested urgency and speed.

Whatever they were doing, Braxiatel now knew, they

specifically needed Bernice Summerfield.

And whatever she was involved in, they were willing to kill to get it.

Braxiatel's subsequent call, to the Yendipp residence, went unanswered. While that worried and angered him, it did not come as a surprise.

'Oh, Benny,' he murmured, 'what have I got you into this time?' He settled back into his chair, his mind racing through the permutations and possibilities. 'I just hope you're safe, wherever you are. And that you know who your friends are.'

7
Everyone Comes to Piccolini's

Bernice Summerfield's diary. Entry for Sunday January 6th 2600.

At least it didn't catch fire. When I came round, apart from the usual bruises and splitting headache I seemed to be reasonably intact. The pod's guidance systems had homed in on the major centre of population, I guess because that's where the most communications traffic is. I wasn't exactly sitting in the middle of Main Street as I clambered out of the battered, scorched shell of the pod. But I was within sight of the city of Kasagrad.

I've got a bit of cash, and my credit is apparently good for the moment (thanks, Brax!). At least until the invasion.

It's a strange atmosphere. Everyone seems to accept that the Fifth Axis is going to invade. It's just a question of when. So far the defence shields have done the job, but there doesn't seem to be any illusion that this is anything but temporary. The government's treated as a lame duck – either they'll surrender, or they'll grant more and more control to the Axis. There's some debate, in hushed voices with furtive looks over the shoulder, as to whether it would be better to go down fighting or to let the government just roll over and play dead. Fifth Axis rule by proxy. Hobson's choice, really.

I've got a room at Piccolini's. It's a bar and bistro-type place really. But they do have some accommodation. Actually, I think I'm the only guest. Not a lot of tourism here these days. But Piccolini's is definitely the place to be. Everyone who's anyone meets here. It's sort of safe, neutral ground I guess. Even the Fifth Axis officers from the local garrison come here.

Not that they call it a garrison. But it's pretty clear these are the troops who will take control when the balloon goes up. No, it's a transit station or something – they're all just on their way somewhere. Yeah, right. They've been on their way somewhere for months.

So it's pretty cosmopolitan here at Piccolini's. Take this evening, for example. I just happened to be in the bar for a while earlier on. They have robot waiters who are pretty attentive. Not very reliable, mind you – can't get the spare parts apparently. Piccolini's always sending the others off to dismantle one that's gone wrong and try to reuse the bits. But for the most part they check with you as you finish one drink and bring you another.

They're a bit creepy actually – humanoid shape and size, but with completely blank faces. No attempt even at a nose-bump, let alone eyes. Just metal. Blank non-staring metal. It's a bit weird to see yourself reflected as you ask for more drinks. Wouldn't have thought it was very good for business, actually – watching your increasingly inarticulate and blurry pleas for further alcohol. But the beer's not too bad, and maybe most people don't make non-eye contact with them. Saves on tipping too. (Oh big doo-dah – maybe I'm meant to tip them. Better watch what everyone else does next time. Hmmm.)

So anyway, I was at my usual table (been here two days, and already they leave it free for me – it's that kind of place). Piccolini was behind the bar, polishing glasses and making conversation. He's pretty good at sharing the opinion of whoever he's listening to. Doesn't talk much himself, which is probably just as well. He's kind of short and plump with a round face and thinning black hair. He keeps his hair oiled back, so it looks even thinner than it really is. I don't think he's really come to terms with the plump thing yet either – his suits are really good quality, but they're all two sizes too small round the waist. The trousers are straining and the jackets wouldn't do up unless you put your knee in his stomach while you pulled the edges together. Not that I'm about to try you understand.

So, who else was in? Well, there's a few guys and a woman who come in most nights (she says on a random sample of two!). They're about my age (maybe ten years younger actually, but I still maintain that's about my age) and they wear sort of trench coats with the collars turned up and sit in a corner whispering. If you go near them, they all start shh-ing each other and look embarrassed and stare at their fingernails and stuff. So it's quite fun to do that every so often. From the way they look when Kendrick comes in, it's pretty obvious they aren't planning ways to help the Fifth Axis guys take over.

Raul Kendrick is the Kommandant or whatever of the Axis troops. It's an unspoken assumption that when the crunch comes, he'll be the one in charge of the invasion and will probably end up running the planet. So everyone hates him, but goes out of their way to be nice and polite. There's a fine line between those who are doing it to avoid trouble, and those who go the extra mile in the hope of coming out of things well. Collaboration before the fact, almost.

They modify their behaviour, well a bit, when Herv Gresham is around. He's some kind of government type and nobody seems to know what his opinion of the situation is. The trench-coat table evidently expect him to roll over as soon as the shooting starts. They have him pegged for an ineffectual wimp. But Kendrick seems pretty wary of him. I've only spoken to Gresham once, and that was just to apologise for getting beer on his sleeve. His fault of course. Well, ninety per cent his fault. He was pretty good about it really. Wasn't just his sleeve you see.

Kendrick's less polite in my experience, but then the difference is that Gresham probably needs all the friends he can get and Kendrick has more than he wants. Normally it would be the other way round. Local-boy Gresham is polite, tall, handsome in a rugged middle-aged and tired sort of way. I think he's pretty shrewd too, actually.

Kendrick is certainly shrewd. And shrew-like. He's shorter than Gresham and fuller of figure, though not a plumpy like Piccolini. Most of it is muscle I reckon. He's always immaculately uniformed. But however smart he is and however smart he looks, it doesn't make up for the eye patch and the scar. The two are related I would guess, since the scar starts on his forehead, then runs under the eye patch and emerges across his cheek. That side – the right side – of his face has a sort of scrunched up look as a result. He limps the same side too. Always has a walking stick with him. It's metal with a skull emblem on the handle. He lays it across the table when he sits down and his hand is never far from it – like it's a threat.

The other obvious difference is that Gresham usually comes alone and drinks alone. Kendrick has an entourage (bodyguard?) of half a dozen or more Axis officers. They all hang on his every word, and laugh when he's laughing. I laughed when he wasn't, that's why he was rude to me. Just because he slipped on some beer I'd spilled and sat down on the floor. I mean, I apologised and everything. I don't know, some people just have no sense of humour do they?

So this is where I'm stuck for the moment. There's no way off this planet, not with the blockade (er, 'trade regulation') going on. The communications are laughably primitive, so I guess I just wait for Brax to come and find me. I can while away the time by looking round for an illegal way of getting away from Kasagrad (then not doing it if there's any sort of risk attached), and by trying to piece together enough from Goram's half of the manuscript to find Rablev's Mislaid Tomb. A bit of fieldwork sounds likes fun, actually. Though I'm not sure what I'll do if I find it. I've a feeling that some – maybe even most – of the people here would actually welcome the end of the world.

All of them are expecting it.

The only person I haven't heard express fear, anxiety and doubt is Piccolini. He just shrugs and says that whatever will happen will happen and until then it's all good for business.

I've a feeling Kendrick might agree with him. But given the business he's obviously in, I somehow don't find that a very comforting thought.

The room was small and hot. Benny tossed her diary into her rucksack and flopped down on the bed. The fan in the ceiling looked as if it was held in place by the cobwebs. Maybe it was the cobwebs, Benny thought, that stopped it from revolving. She knew every cobweb by name now. Only two days, but no end in sight. She needed to do something to keep herself occupied. Something other than sitting in the bar and watching other people.

After a couple of minutes, Benny levered herself into a sitting position and reached down for her rucksack. It was late and she was tired, but the fact that she had spent another whole day effectively doing nothing was depressing. Well, doing nothing other than trying to consume enough alcohol to make the ceiling fan revolve.

She fished through the contents for the holosphere. Her hand closed on something that seemed the right shape and she pulled it out – Joseph. She tossed him aside, and he rolled across the bed covers before rising unsteadily into the air.

'I'm not in the mood for talking,' Benny said before Joseph could say anything. He bobbed up towards the ceiling and seemed to be examining the cobwebs. Benny was tempted to ask him if he could fix the fan. But she was pretty sure she knew the answer, so she kept silent.

The portable reader was a roll of active matrix screen that Benny flattened out and propped against the holosphere. It used osmotic data induction to draw the information out of the holographic storage and display it on the screen. The screen was touch-sensitised and had a built-in voice parser. She was all set now. All set to go through Goram's half of the Doomsday Manuscript with a fine-toothed comb and start assembling the evidence. If anyone could unravel the mystery, then it was Professor Bernice Summerfield.

Who was she kidding, Benny wondered as she stifled a yawn.

She propped the screen against the sphere on the cabinet by her bed. She turned to the photograph showing Jason in the background, and enlarged it so that he was in the centre of the screen. The left half of the man in front of Jason stared back obliviously, his huge bushy moustache seeming to thrust forward from the screen, a slash of red at the edge of the picture. Jason was still in shadow, but she could see him clearly enough.

She lay back on the pillow, head turned so that she could see the screen, could see Jason looking back at her. And cried herself to sleep.

Benny woke in a good mood. She was determined now to take a proper look at the manuscript and deduce whatever she could. If nothing else, she could get on with some fieldwork, maybe hook up with some local archaeologists. There would be libraries and records offices and museums. No end of research possibilities. Whether she was really looking for the Lost Tomb of Rablev or for evidence of Jason, it didn't matter. What mattered was keeping busy.

She caught sight of Joseph still loitering amongst the cobwebs as she poured herself coffee from the scummy percolator on the dressing table.

'Okay, Joseph,' she called up at him, 'you can come down now, I'm dressed. And I'm not that modest where overgrown diary management systems are concerned anyway.'

'I beg your –' Joseph began.

But Benny cut him off with a raised hand. 'Right then, to business.'

'Business?' There was just a hint of anxiety mixed in with his usual nasal intonation.

Benny ignored him, and continued: 'I want you to clear my calendar for the next week. All meetings cancelled, hold all calls.'

'But you don't have any –'

'Good, glad to see you're on board already.' Benny nodded enthusiastically. 'Now, I want you to set aside an hour every evening for socialization and researching the local hostelries.'

'I'm afraid,' Joseph said as he bobbed just out of Benny's reach, 'that my storage is –'

'Better make that three hours every evening,' Benny went on. 'A girl's got to eat as well, you know.'

'I am aware that biological –'

'And don't keep interrupting,' she warned him. 'The rest of the time, all week, I want assigned in equal and efficient parts to the following tasks.' She held up her hand, ready to count them off on her fingers. 'Let's see, local museums are probably a good start. Get into the rhythm of it. Soak up the local atmosphere and history. Then there's –'

This time Joseph cut her off. 'I'm sorry,' he insisted, 'but I can't.' His apology was a shrill squeak of embarrassment.

'Can't?' She stared at him, and he revolved and bobbed in an uncomfortable-looking way. 'I know you're useless at most things, but I was led to believe that managing a calendar was the one task that's actually within your capabilities.' She cocked her head to one side. 'Perhaps I have been misinformed?'

'It is, normally, yes.' Joseph started on a short tour of the small room, dipping in and out of the corners. 'But my available storage is currently extremely limited due to your other requests.'

'Doesn't matter,' Benny said. 'I sort of guessed I'd be better off doing it myself anyway.' She grabbed her rucksack and hoisted it over her shoulder. 'Why don't you just have a little lie down or whatever you do and –' She stopped, mouth still open, and peered closely at the animated sphere as it bobbed past. 'How much storage do you actually have?' she demanded. 'I mean it must be fifty terabytes or so at least.'

Joseph coughed with pride. 'Rather more than that, actually.'

'And it's all being used,' Benny said before he could go on. 'Coping with my other requests.'

'Indeed.'

She sucked in her cheeks and nodded thoughtfully. 'Just out of curiosity really,' she said, 'could you remind me what those other requests are? I mean they must be pretty significant to use so much of your capacity, but strangely I don't recall asking you to do anything very much. I wasn't aware that you could do anything very much.'

'Your exact instructions were,' Joseph said, clearing his throat, '"If you could download that into your local memory, we'd at least have something to show for all this".'

Benny pulled off her rucksack and sat down on the edge of the bed. 'Remind me,' she said slowly, 'where I was when I said that.'

'In your room at Munroe Hennessy's house.'

Benny thought about this. 'And so that's what you did? You downloaded it into your local memory where it is now consuming almost all the available space.'

'As you instructed.' He sounded smug now.

'Excellent. Good. Well done.' She gave him a huge thumbs up. 'And what exactly are we talking about here?'

'Video data, from the Hennessy security cameras.'

'Ah.' Benny wondered if she was willing to risk more of the scummy coffee. She had convinced herself that one cup a day, first thing in the morning, couldn't do her too much damage. But a second cup might be pushing it.

'In particular,' Joseph went on, 'you were interested in: "useful insert shots of his half of the Doomsday Manuscript".'

'I think,' Benny said, 'that, if you'll pardon the expression, you'd better show me what you've got.'

Benny had woken late. But even so, she was surprised to find that it was well into what she regarded as lunchtime before she had finished viewing the footage. Using the screen from the holosphere, Joseph was able to show Benny the output from Hennessy's security cameras. He had, he was evidently proud to report, scanned through the video archive on Hennessy's main computer storage system, and taken a copy of any frames that seemed at all related to the Doomsday Manuscript.

'It's time-stamped data, you see,' he explained gleefully, 'so my scheduling protocols are able to access and assimilate it.'

They went through it at terrific speed since there was so

much data. Occasionally Benny asked Joseph to pause or go back, but for the most part she let it wash over her. She was stunned, and amazed, and disappointed.

She was stunned at her good fortune, at Joseph's useful – for once – interpretation of her chance remark. She was amazed that there was so much footage that included a view of some sort of the manuscript being accessed. And she was disappointed that most of the shots were of no use at all. If only, she thought, a camera had recorded Hennessy going through the thing page by page at bedtime. But she decided this was probably too much to have hoped for and she should be happy with what she had.

So instead of griping, she said: 'Well done, Joseph. This is really great. I think that someone who knew what they were doing, and who had the right equipment and expertise could go through and probably get a half decent image of just about every missing half-page.' She hoped there weren't too many qualifiers in there to dampen the effect. 'Then they could put it together with the Goram half we already have and Bob's your uncle.' She let out a long breath. 'All we have to do now is find that someone.'

Joseph spun happily behind the screen which was frozen on a distorted over-the-shoulder shot of a screen display of part of a blurred map. 'That does sound eminently achievable, Professor Summerfield.'

'Benny,' she corrected him automatically.

'But I do have one question.'

'Oh?' She looked up from the screen.

'How do you know his name will be Bob?'

She decided to start with the anti-Axis drinking club, as she thought of them. Sure enough there were two of them – the woman and one of the men – sitting at their usual corner table and trying to look innocent and inconspicuous. The man had long dark hair that could have done with a wash. The woman looked like there was something that smelled nasty stuck under her nose – the rest of her face seemed to be trying to escape from it.

True to form, they immediately stopped their conversation as Benny approached. One of the blank-faced waiter robots was stood behind them, presumably expecting a drinks order.

'Get us a beer, would you?' Benny told the robot as she arrived at the table.

It stared at her, so far as she could tell, since it had no eyes, but made no effort to move.

'Beer,' she said again deliberately. 'In a glass. To drink.' She made raising a glass and drinking gestures at the thing until it seemed to get the message and went reluctantly on its way. Benny sighed and turned to the man and woman at the table. They were watching her in a way that made it obvious they wanted her to go away.

'Can't get the staff these days,' Benny told them brightly. 'May I sit down?' She didn't wait for an answer because she knew what it would be, but pulled out a chair and shoved her rucksack under it. The pianist in the opposite corner of the bar struck up a happy melody that counterpointed their expressions.

'There's a free table over there.' The man pointed across the room.

It was half empty, so Benny was willing to believe him without turning to look. 'I've no doubt there is.' She smiled. 'But it's the scintillating company I'm after.' She waited for them to exchange glances before adding: 'But failing that, I wanted to talk to you two.'

The robot was back with a beer. It set down the bottle in front of Benny and stepped back deferentially.

'It's no good, you know,' the woman said, sneering.

'The beer? Oh I know.' Benny clicked her fingers and beckoned the robot back out of the shadows behind the table. 'I did ask for a glass, actually. Memory chips a bit frail are they?'

It stared at her again in its blank way.

Benny stared back. 'Please?' she offered.

The robot turned and stalked off. Benny watched it in amusement. It actually seemed put out at having to work. She could almost swear it had let out a sigh of annoyance before it went. 'Where were we?' she wondered out loud. 'Oh yes, I was after some advice actually.'

'It won't work,' the woman said. Her lip was curling dangerously. 'Kendrick's tried to infiltrate us before, you know.'

'Really?' Benny took a swig of beer from the bottle. She wiped her mouth with the back of her hand. 'Was he any more welcome here than I am?'

'His sort aren't welcome anywhere,' the man said. He kept his voice low and menacing.

'Well, I'd probably agree with you there,' Benny admitted. The robot was back with a glass. Benny frowned, looked at the bottle in her hand, then at the glass. 'It's all right, I don't need that now,' she said.

The robot slammed the glass down on the table so hard she thought it might shatter.

'Just get lost, girl. All right?' the woman said sharply.

'Girl?' Benny put her beer down next to the glass. 'Girl? I'm a professor of archaeology I'll have you know.' She leaned across the table. 'And I'm probably several years older than you.'

The woman laughed. Actually laughed. 'And the rest,' she snorted.

Benny took a moment to recover her calm. She took another swig of beer. 'Any more of your lip,' she said, 'and you'll have trouble drinking.' Before they could work this out, she went on: 'I just want some help, all right? I'm working on something that is of vital importance to your world. I'm not with the Axis, and I don't care for them at all. Though it may be that they are more willing to help me than you are.'

'So what do you want?' the man asked. He still managed to make it sound like a threat.

'I reckon you probably do forged papers, permits, ration

books or whatever,' Benny said. She almost laughed out loud at the way they shuffled uncomfortably and looked at each other. 'In the interests of maintaining Kasagrad's independence of course.'

'So what if we... did?' the woman asked.

'So, I need someone who's good at putting data together. Taking bits and pieces to create a whole. Image enhancement. That sort of thing.' Benny took another long pull at the beer and drained the bottle. 'Seemed to me that would be the sort of thing you were into.'

The main door to Piccolini's opened, then slammed shut and they all turned to look. Raul Kendrick was striding across towards his usual table, several officers in greatcoats following in his wake.

'Kendrick,' the man at the table hissed. He made it sound like an expletive.

'I'll tell you the sort of thing we're into,' the woman said. Her voice was louder than previously – at normal volume rather than hushed and conspiratorial. 'We're into keeping our independence no matter what our weak, corrupted government might decide. We're into liberty and human rights.'

Her voice was rising. People at neighbouring tables turned to watch. Benny smiled weakly at them and shrugged as the woman continued with her passionate outburst. 'We're into retaining what we're entitled to, self-determination and democracy.'

'Ilsa!' the man hissed urgently as Kendrick swung round in his seat to stare across at them.

'We're into fighting for it if we have to.' She stood up, her chair falling over as it shot out from behind her. 'And we're not into being dictated to by foreign powers. We won't be bullied, or blockaded, or blackmailed, or invaded.'

Kendrick was leaning back in his chair, an expression of amusement seeping out from under his eye patch as he watched her.

'I get the picture,' Benny assured the woman. 'No

problem. I'll ask elsewhere. Really.'

But the woman ignored her. 'Play it, play it now,' she called across the room.

The pianist half stood up from his stool, his hands making a 'who, me?' gesture. But her stare was too much for him, and he sank back on to the stool. There was a general murmuring from round the room now, a subcurrent of noise. 'Play it, go on... why not... it's a free planet. Still. For the moment. Play it while you can...'

The pianist shot a quick glance at Kendrick, who was still staring at the woman standing opposite Benny. Then he turned towards the bar where Piccolini was leaning heavily on the counter.

The big man shrugged, sighed, shook his head. The pianist interpreted this as permission, and began to play.

The music was lilting and uplifting. Melodic, but with a strong base line. As soon as the music started, what conversations were still happening stopped. The young man next to Benny stood up, straight and erect, like a soldier standing to attention. Gradually other people were standing up too. Before long it seemed like only Benny and the people at Kendrick's table were still seated. Even Piccolini was standing as tall as he ever did behind the bar.

Kendrick was staring at Benny, his expression a mixture of amusement and interest. Benny returned his stare. He raised his glass to her, his one eyebrow lifting slightly. Benny smiled back thinly, and stood up.

There was a silence when the music finished. As if someone had said something they shouldn't in a quiet moment at a funeral. Then gradually people sat down and conversations resumed. Benny sat down too. The man and woman at the table seemed to be avoiding catching her eye. They were also not looking at each other. Perhaps they were just beginning to think about what they had done. Whatever that was, Benny thought.

But she did not have time to ask them, as Kendrick was standing beside her suddenly. His walking stick slapped down on the table, the skull device on the handle staring at Benny with sightless eyes.

'You like the Kasagrad anthem, then?' His voice was rolled in gravel.

The woman made to answer him, but Kendrick put his hand up to stop her. It was a sudden, violent, impersonal gesture that had immediate effect. 'I was talking to Professor Summerfield,' he said.

Benny's throat went dry. She had told nobody her full name. Just Benny – that was all she was here. 'It's stirring stuff,' she said, forcing a smile. 'It seemed respectful to stand,' she added. 'I thought.' She hoped she got enough of an accusation into her look and her tone.

'Did you now.' He nodded as if he had known this all along. 'Personally, I think it's rather old fashioned, don't you?' He turned to look at Ilsa and the man. 'Had its day, I would think.'

'We won't ask you to join us,' Benny said before they could comment. She could see the anger rising in the woman's face like a thermometer. The man was shifting uncomfortably in his seat.

'Good,' Kendrick shot back. 'That will save you the embarrassment of my refusal.' So saying he pulled his stick from the table and swung round.

One of the robot waiters was passing, carrying a tray of drinks. It stopped abruptly as Kendrick stepped in front of it. So abruptly that one of the bottles fell forwards. It perched for a moment on the edge of the tray then toppled to the ground. As it fell, it splashed beer over Kendrick's chest.

He looked down at the frothy trail on his coat. His face contorted in anger, the eye patch quivering as the remains of the face beneath moved. Then he lashed out with his walking stick. The blow caught the waiter across its blank face, and the robot staggered back. The sound was an echoing ringing of metal on metal. The waiter teetered like the bottle had before collapsing backwards on to an empty table. The wood splintered and snapped, and the table fell apart, its legs splayed under the heavy robot's carcass.

The waiter struggled to get up. Servos strained and hissed. Its hands groped at the air. There was a fizzing sound from somewhere behind the face plate.

Kendrick stepped forward and placed the tip of his walking stick on the joint between the neck and the body. With a grunt of effort he thrust it deep into the metal shell. A shower of dark viscous liquid erupted from the puncture point, spraying over the robot's thrashing body. Then it slowed to a dribble as the robot's movements stilled.

'What is going on here?' Piccolini demanded as he barrelled his way through from the bar. He caught sight of Kendrick. 'Is there a problem, sir?' His tone was mollified.

'Not any more,' Kendrick assured him, dusting down his coat.

'You've killed it,' Benny said out loud, astounded at the violence and anger of the attack.

'What a singularly romantic notion,' Kendrick said, wiping the oily end of his stick on a napkin. 'It was just an automaton. It was never alive.' His thick lips drew back in a bloodless smile. 'Unfortunately.'

'Irreparable,' Piccolini complained as he examined the shattered remains of his waiter. He beckoned to another of the blank-faced robots to come over. 'Take it away,' he said. 'Disassemble it and save whatever parts can be reused.' He straightened up, shaking his head in annoyance.

Kendrick was gone, his entourage following him out, leaving their drinks in various stages of being drunk on the table. The man and woman at Benny's table had also left, Benny saw as she looked round. In fact, the whole bar seemed to have thinned out rather. Too much excitement for one afternoon, she decided.

The clientele who were left made way for Piccolini's ample form as he went back to the bar. Benny raised her beer bottle in the hope of extracting a final few drops of liquid. As she tilted her head back, a figure at the back of the bar, at a table on his own, caught her eye. He was shaking his head, as if to admonish her, as if to say: 'Well, I wouldn't have done that.'

Jason.

It was Jason.

For a split-second it was Jason. Then she saw that it wasn't actually anything like Jason. Not even close. It was Herv Gresham, the man from the government, though Benny had not been able to discover what it was he did exactly.

She put down the bottle and wondered why she had been so certain he was Jason. The impression had only lasted a split-second. Just as she looked across the bar. She screwed up her eyes and tried to recreate the illusion.

And her heart stopped.

It wasn't Gresham. It was the man at the table between where Benny was and where Gresham sat. Looking past him had done it. Had reminded her of the torn photograph in the Doomsday Manuscript. Gresham was sitting where she had subconsciously expected Jason to be.

As she watched in shocked disbelief the man got up, unrolled a few banknotes and left them on the table, and started towards the door. Benny's attention was fixed on his weather-beaten face, on the huge, red, bushy moustache that stretched across it.

It was the man standing in front of Jason in the photograph. In the photograph taken four hundred years ago. And he looked not a day older.

Almost before she realized it, he was across the bar and leaving by the main door. Benny ran after him, knocking a chair aside as she ran, catching her rucksack on another as she dragged it behind her, hardly noticing. She shot out of the door, dazzled for a moment by the bright sunlight outside. She shielded her eyes with her hand and looked first one way along the street, then the other.

But the man had gone.

8
Dumb Waiter

There seemed to be three possibilities. Benny thought them through as she made her way back through the bar and towards her room. First, and most plausible, was a case of mistaken identity. She had fallen asleep staring at the picture, and when she saw someone with a moustache that was vaguely similar to the guy in the photograph her mind leapt to an illogical conclusion.

Despite being the most plausible explanation, she discarded it at once. Benny was certain of what she had seen. The fact that she had studied that photo so intently, every detail of it, only served to reinforce her opinion that this had been the same man.

Which left her with two less probable explanations. The first of these was that the man was incredibly long-lived. It was the same person, but he had not aged in over four hundred years. Or shaved. Even if he was ultra-conservative in his opinion about his appearance, this seemed slightly less likely than the final option.

Time travel. Somehow and for some reason the man had travelled forward four hundred years. Maybe this was indeed his own time and he had travelled back to get his picture taken. Whatever. Though this was the least possible choice, it was the one that appealed most to Benny.

The reason for that was Jason. If he had been there, four hundred years ago, then he had travelled back in time somehow to get there. And the presence here today of Mr Moustachio meant that it was possible that Jason might travel forward to the present. Might turn up at any moment at Piccolini's.

Implausible it might be, but it was the option that gave Benny most hope. It was a renewed motivation for her researches. Despite having lost the man outside the bar, despite the fact that Raul Kendrick somehow knew who she was, she felt on a high.

Until she opened the door to her room.

Luckily it was a small room, so there was not much scope for making a mess. But someone had tried. Benny's possessions, such as they were, had been turned out of drawers and cupboards. The bed had been stripped and the covers and sheets dumped in a heap on the floor. The windows were open, the curtains flapping in the afternoon breeze. And the bathroom was an absolute tip. Which meant, Benny thought, that they probably hadn't searched in there – it was exactly as she'd left it.

'No prizes for guessing what they were after,' Benny muttered to herself as she closed the windows. She looked round the room, wondering where to start. And decided that back in the bar was the best place. If nothing else, she still had to find someone to help edit Joseph's video clips into shape, and she could also ask about Mr Moustachio.

Before she left, she took the holosphere of the Doomsday Manuscript from her rucksack and stuffed it into the middle of the bundle of sheets and blankets. They were not likely, whoever they were, to come back and search again. Especially if it looked as if Benny had not even discovered their first intrusion.

She hesitated a moment, wondering whether to hide Joseph with the holosphere. It was tempting, if only to hear his muffled opinion on the matter. But there was a saying about eggs and baskets that sprang to mind, and Benny decided to keep him in the rucksack.

The evening was beginning to draw in. A ground-car was waiting in the alley at the back of Piccolini's. A figure darted across from the back door and got into the car. At once the vehicle pulled away. Its lights only came on when it joined the main highway through the city, melded with the early evening flow of traffic.

The driver said nothing. The passenger in the back seat sat

immobile for several minutes. The blank, metal face angled towards the floor as if the robot waiter was looking at its feet. Then it seemed to come to life, head snapping up, white-gloved hands reaching for its face plate and sliding back along the cheeks, fumbling for the release mechanism.

The whole of the face plate detached from the back of the head, coming away in the gloved hands. Bryn Lavers blinked, and drew a long, deep breath of unfiltered air. 'That's better,' he said quietly, as much as anything to hear the sound of his own voice. 'You don't have anything to eat do you?' he asked the driver. 'I've just done an eight hour shift and I'm starving.'

The Axis barracks was a large, low building. An unimaginative square block of concrete and steel. It was ringed by a high wall topped with electro-razor wire. The main gates were blast-proof and swung open ponderously as the vehicle approached.

In the back of the car, Lavers finished the chocolate bar the driver had given him. He was still hungry. He was also incredibly thirsty. And he would have to be back at Piccolini's soon. The robot waiter that he kept hidden in a cupboard to take his place when he wasn't there was getting temperamental. If Piccolini had it retired before he got back that could create a problem. He would have to replace one of the others somehow, and he didn't know their command codes.

Kendrick was waiting for him. Being the Kommandant, he had an enormous office. The Fifth Axis flag hung beside his desk, taking up most of the wall. On the desk, angled so that visitors could see it, was a signed hologram of the Imperator himself. On the wall behind the desk was another, far larger, portrait of the Imperator. His piercing blue eyes seemed to stare accusingly at Lavers as he made his report.

'I'm sorry about the incident this afternoon,' Lavers said. He was wringing his gloved hands behind his back as he spoke.

Kendrick waved his apology away. 'Make this quick,' he

said. 'I don't have a lot of time. Have you found it?'

'It isn't in her room. I checked most thoroughly.'

'Where else is there?' Kendrick demanded.

'Well, she does carry a rucksack.'

'A rucksack?' Kendrick's single eye was staring at him as intently as the Imperator's image.

'She keeps it with her. Always. I have watched.'

Kendrick drew a deep breath. 'You're sure it isn't in her room?'

'Absolutely, sir.'

Kendrick nodded. 'And you put everything back exactly as it was? So she won't know that we're looking for the holosphere?'

Lavers gulped. He felt the blood drain from his face. 'Of course,' he managed to stammer.

Kendrick leaned back in his chair, swinging slightly back and forth as he watched Lavers closely. 'Of course,' he echoed, his voice quiet but laced with menace.

'Er, the rucksack,' Lavers went on quickly. 'Do you want me to try to –'

'Your job is to observe and report. Let me worry about Professor Summerfield's rucksack.' Kendrick leaned forward again, shuffled papers on his desk and picked up a pen. 'Anything else?'

'The woman, the one who had the Anthem played…'

'What about her?' He did not look up.

'She is in charge of the group, it seems. They listen to her, respect her.'

Kendrick did look up now. The skin round his eye patch twitched, as if the eye behind was winking. 'Good. Well done, Lavers.'

'Her name is Ilsa Deveraux. She has a flat on the Bergenstrasse. Above number twenty-six.'

Kendrick laid down the pen and tapped his fingertips together thoughtfully. 'Perhaps it is time to make a point,' he said quietly.

'You won't –' Lavers broke off and licked his lips. His

mouth was getting even more dry.

'Let me worry about what I will and won't do,' Kendrick snapped angrily. He pressed a button set into the surface of his desk. 'Ask my Adjutant to come in. Lavers is leaving, pay him as usual and then get him back to Piccolini's.' Kendrick looked up at Lavers again. 'You just concentrate on your own health. Let me worry about other people's.'

Lavers swallowed dryly. 'Yes, sir. Of course sir.' He shuffled his feet, anxious to be gone before Kendrick's Adjutant arrived.

Piccolini seemed like the best person to start with. Since the bar was relatively quiet early in the evening, he was leaning on the counter listening to the piano. The pianist had gone for a break, but the piano seemed not to mind and was tinkling out a mournful melody on its own.

'Do you actually need the pianist?' Benny asked him. It was as good an opening as any, and rather better than 'When do you want next week's rent?'

'It's a credibility thing,' Piccolini said. 'And old Andravio isn't bad.' He nodded at the piano, 'He's nearly as good as the instrument itself.'

'And you need the credibility?' Benny asked.

Piccolini smiled. He didn't often smile, and Benny had never seen him grin. This was probably the closest she would get. 'The money comes in handy,' he said. 'It's not my credibility I'm talking about.'

'The money?' She was about five minutes behind him. When she caught up, she laughed. 'You mean…?'

Piccolini nodded. 'He gets bookings all over the city on the strength of his reputation here.' He shrugged. 'So Andravio pays me, I let him sit at the piano, the piano entertains the punters. Occasionally he has to do a request and actually play for himself. Like this afternoon when your friend Ilsa decided to play silly-bees.'

'She's not my friend,' Benny said. Piccolini had slapped a bottle of beer on the bar without mentioning it. Benny knew from experience just to take it and not to thank him. 'I was after some information, actually.'

'You'll be after a coffin if Kendrick sees you with her, actually,' he snapped back. It was not ill-meant.

Benny snorted. 'You don't really believe Kendrick would go that far?' She hadn't meant it to be a question, but as she said it, as she saw how serious he really was, she found her voice rising unbidden at the end of the sentence.

'I'll tell you what I believe,' he said quietly, checking all round to assure himself they were alone at the bar. 'I believe this planet is going to hell in a handcart. And Kendrick's right at the front whipping the guys who're doing the pulling.' He helped himself to a bottle of beer. Benny had not seen him do that before. 'And the guys doing the pulling are probably our own government. Better to be in the Axis than in our graves, that's what they think.' He took a long swig of beer. 'I'm not convinced they've got that right.'

Benny thought about this. 'What about resistance?' she asked quietly. 'What about standing up to them? To the Fifth Axis and to the puppet government?'

He was leaning across the bar, his mouth close to her ear. 'If Ilsa Deveraux, for all her contacts and bravado, if the best she can do to hold off an invasion is have the Anthem played in a second rate bar by a third rate pianist, then we don't have a prayer.'

'Oh come on,' Benny told him sternly. 'Don't be so defeatist.' She held up the beer bottle, using it to punctuate her point. 'There's nothing second rate about this place.'

He appreciated that, and it seemed to restore something of his earlier good mood. 'So what did you want from Ilsa?'

'Information, that's all.'

'You should have come to me,' he told her.

'You were busy.' She shrugged. 'And I wasn't sure it was information you'd want to part with.'

'No harm in asking.' He lowered his voice again. 'Not yet, anyway.' A customer approached the bar – some of them, usually the regulars, still preferred to deal with Piccolini direct rather than trust the waiters.

'Two things,' Benny confided in Piccolini when he returned.

He nodded. 'We'll be getting busy soon, so better make it quick.'

'First, the guy with the moustache.'

'Mikey,' Piccolini said. 'Don't know much more about him. He comes in a lot. Drinks a lot. Loses a lot at the casino, I hear. Always on the lookout for a bit of extra cash.'

'He'll be here tonight?' Benny asked eagerly.

'Maybe. Sometimes we don't see him for a few days. You can never tell. What's the other thing?' he asked. 'You weren't expecting Ilsa to tell you about Mikey.'

'No, I wasn't,' she admitted. 'I was hoping she knew a decent counterfeiter. Someone who puts together data from different sources and creates a document.'

Piccolini smiled thinly. 'You after a ration book or an ID card or something?'

'Nothing illegal,' Benny assured him. He laughed aloud at that. 'No, really. I just want some help putting some data from different sources together. It's an historical document,' she told him.

'Is it?' He obviously was not convinced. 'Well, doesn't matter,' he said. 'The answer's the same whatever it is. You need to talk to Georgia Salis, she's the best there is. I can make a good guess at her address.' He leaned forward again as someone else came over to the bar and stood waiting for Piccolini's attention. He whispered the address, then added: 'We call her...' His eyes flicked to and fro as he prepared to finished the sentence: 'Georgia the –'

'Georgia the Forger?' Benny suggested.

Piccolini was stunned. His eyes widened and his eyebrows knitted together. 'How did you know that?'

'Lucky guess,' she assured him. 'I have a knack for the apposite epithet.'

Nobody on the Bergenstrasse saw or heard anything. Not

until afterwards. The street was almost deserted and nearly dark when the tall blond-haired man let himself into the flat above number twenty-six.

He found her at the terminal, checking her messages. She was midway through typing a reply when the blade sliced down into her windpipe. It didn't kill her, just took away her ability to shout for help. He left her crawling, bleeding across the carpet as he downloaded the contents of her local storage onto a holo-disk. Then he slipped the disk into his coat pocket, got up from the machine, and kicked her hard in the stomach.

He sat watching her for ten minutes before he got bored. Then he grabbed her hair and pulled her head back. She was almost at the door. The skin tightened round the hole in her throat, forcing a bead of blood through the narrowing gap. Her breathing was a rasping retch of sound by now. He looked into her terrified eyes, then drew the stiletto blade across the taut windpipe, stepping aside as he dropped her to avoid the blood.

He dumped the body out of the back window into an alley. She would be found by morning, he knew. Sooner than if he just left her locked in the flat. And it would be apparent to all that her death was far from quick and anything but painless.

But then that was the point.

The address that Piccolini had given her was the other side of the main street market. Benny knew the area and was confident she could find the right road even in the dark.

She was almost at market when the youth attacked her. Along this street, she knew, was the area where during the day the market stalls were set up. But now they were deserted, skeletal structures of scaffolding and planks standing stark against the dim light of those street lamps that still worked.

As Benny stood taking in the bizarre sight, a figure leapt out of the darkness of a doorway. For a moment Benny saw his young face in the insipid aura of the nearest lamp. Then it was shadowed again as he barrelled into her, knocking her flying. A long thin knife blade glinted a moment, then as quickly as he had come, he was gone.

Benny struggled to her feet and stared down the street after him. She could hear his booted feet slapping on the cobbles long after she lost sight of him. Only when she looked down did she realize that her rucksack was gone.

'I hope you like dirty laundry,' she shouted after him. 'You've got my second best knickers in there you know.' She shook her head, blew out a long exhalation of relief that she was unhurt and turned back towards the market.

'Knickers!' she shouted suddenly into the empty street. How was she going to manage without any knickers? And at the same instant she remembered that Joseph was also inside the rucksack. 'Typical,' she mumbled to herself. Probably he'd be able to find his way back to Piccolini's. Probably. But she wasn't sure she could take the risk.

She set off at a desultory trot after her attacker. There was not much hope of finding him, she knew. But if he opened the rucksack and let Joseph out then maybe she would hear the protestations.

Benny found the man quicker than she had dared expect or hope. He was in the next street. He was lying in the street, in the middle of a pool of light cast by the lamp above, Benny's rucksack beside him.

Had he slipped? Slipped and fallen? Tripped over the rucksack perhaps – Benny had done that herself a few times. She approached cautiously, expecting him at any moment to roll over, get to his feet and run off again. Maybe shoving her aside or knifing her for good measure in the process.

But he remained absolutely still.

Deathly still.

It was when she stepped in it that Benny got really worried. Her foot slipped and she nearly fell. Her first thought was that this was where the man had fallen – this was what had caused him to slip. But when she stooped to examine the slippery patch on the ground, even as she reached for the strap of her rucksack, she saw that it was blood. The man's blood. Flowing freely still from somewhere underneath him.

Grabbing the rucksack, Benny leapt to her feet. Just as another figure stepped from the shadows beside the body. A figure in a dark combat suit. A figure that moved with the threatening fluidity of a cat.

A figure Benny knew she had last seen struggling along a docking tube between two spaceships.

'Benny,' the figure breathed. The voice was surprisingly soft, sibilant. 'I'm so glad you're here.'

'Yeah,' Benny said. 'I bet.' She was already turning, running, swinging her rucksack on to her back.

Only when she was three streets away did she even pause to look behind her. The street was empty. Cautiously, slowly, warily, she made her way to the address that Piccolini had given her and knocked tentatively at the door.

Georgia Salis, alias Georgia the Forger, turned out to be a middle-aged woman with a mass of greying hair who was almost as wide as she was tall. She was sending two teenage children to bed when Benny arrived, and asked her to make herself coffee and wait in the kitchen. Since this promised to be the best coffee Benny had found since she arrived, she wasn't too put out.

When Georgia appeared, halfway through the second mug, she looked ruffled and hassled and tired.

'So what's your story?' she asked. 'Need more coupons? Change of identity? Ticket for the opera?'

Benny hoiked Joseph out of her rucksack and showed Georgia some of the footage. She described the Doomsday Manuscript she had hidden in her bedclothes, and was relieved and gratified to see that the woman grew first quiet, then pensive, then enthusiastic.

'I'm making no promises you understand,' she told Benny. 'There are some issues here that I need to work through.'

Benny had no idea what she meant, probably something to do with how much she could get out of it. 'Fine,' she said. 'So what's the next step?'

'I want to see the other half of the manuscript,' Georgia told her, making more coffee. 'I want to see for myself if it's what I think it is.'

'You mean you'd rather not put it all together if it means the end of the world?' Benny asked with a grin, accepting another mug of coffee.

'Something like that,' Georgia said. 'I guess,' she added quietly, 'it depends on what you mean by the end of the world.' She glanced at the ceiling. 'I have two kids to look after,' she said.

Again, Benny assumed she was thinking about the money.

They were back at Benny's room at Piccolini's. Georgia was using a technique that Benny wasn't familiar with to split the screen so that it showed Joseph's video material on one side, and the Goram half of the manuscript on the other.

The video side was frozen on a clear shot of half a page of Lacey's manuscript. Georgia had zoomed in on the page, enhanced the resolution, anti-aliased the jaggies and cleaned up the pixelation. On the left side of the screen was the matching page from Goram's manuscript. You could see where the join should be. You could read across from one to the other and get the sense of it.

It would work, Benny told herself. Yes. It would work. She could feel the elation and trepidation and excitement welling in her stomach as she watched Georgia move the video forward to another relatively clear page.

Again, Georgia searched through the Goram manuscript until she came across a match for the other half of the page. She lined them up, and peered closely at the screen.

'I thought so,' she said quietly as she examined them. 'Where did you get this?' she asked.

'Does it matter?' Benny said.

Georgia shrugged. 'I don't know.' She quickly paged

through more of the Goram manuscript, pausing for a moment on the picture of the torn man with the moustache and Jason in the shadows. 'I will tell you this though,' she said, turning to face Benny, 'these don't match.'

'What?' Benny sat down heavily on the bed. 'What do you mean?' she demanded.

'Oh they're close. But there are sections missing from this,' she tapped the Goram side of the screen. 'There are pages in the video data that have no equivalent here. And equally, there are discrepancies. There are sections in your holosphere that just don't fit properly with the video equivalent.'

'But, what does that mean?' Benny said, more to herself than to Georgia.

The older woman answered anyway. 'I'll tell you what it means,' she began with a slight smile.

She got no further. The door to the room crashed open and they both turned, startled, as several figures in uniform marched in.

'Not again,' Georgia said, annoyed. 'You've got nothing on me this time. I'm helping out with some perfectly legal archaeology work. Nothing to interest the security militia.'

'That's right,' Benny said quickly. 'She's helping me.'

'That's good.' The voice was deep and sonorous. Herv Gresham stepped through the uniformed figures and smiled at Benny. 'Because it's you we want.' He nodded to the nearest of the militia, who grabbed Benny tightly by the arm.

'Hey!' she shouted, struggling to pull free. But he held her very firmly.

'Georgia,' Gresham acknowledged politely. 'I doubt if anything you do is actually legal, and it is most certainly of interest.' Without waiting for a reply, he turned and marched from the room, beckoning for the militia men to bring Benny after him.

'Keep working on it,' Benny shouted over her shoulder as she was marched out. 'I'll see you later.'

She saw Georgia's face, lined with sadness, as the door closed. She just caught the woman's quiet words before they were cut off: 'I doubt it.'

It was dark, so Benny saw nothing of the Citadel save for a stark, angular silhouette towering over the landscape. She caught little of the interior either as she was rushed through the main doors, down corridors and steps and brought at last to a heavy wooden door braced with steel bands.

Gresham had left them at Piccolini's, probably to get himself a drink, Benny thought with some annoyance. The militia men said not a word the whole time Benny was with them. So by the time she reached the door, she wasn't bothering to ask questions any more.

One of them pushed the door open. The room beyond was lit by a single hanging bulb, and looked like a cell. The walls were heavy stone, running with damp. It smelled like a public toilet on a hot day during a cleaners' strike. There was a plain wooden table in the middle of the floor, two chairs arranged beside it. Benny saw all this as she was pushed roughly inside.

There was a figure in the room too. A slim, lithe figure dressed in a black combat suit. A figure that moved like a cat as it paced up and down, evidently waiting for Benny to arrive. As the door slammed shut, the figure turned, and Benny saw that it was a woman, her hair cut short. Like a schoolboy, she thought. And at the same moment, recognition dawned.

'You!'

'Yes, Professor Summerfield.' She gestured for Benny to sit on one of the chairs. 'I've been looking forward to having a talk with you.' Luci Yendipp sat down on the other chair and stared at Benny across the table.

9
Faking Life and Cheating Death

'I must apologise for the accommodation,' Luci said. Her nose wrinkled in a way that suggested she wasn't entirely at home with the smell.

'Oh, must you?' Benny said lightly. 'As cells go, this really isn't that bad you know. I'm an expert. Believe me.' She folded her arms and tried to assume a nonchalant devil-may-care attitude. But the smell was getting to her too.

'I tried to speak to you before. Several times.' Her tone was reasonable, friendly. 'I'm sorry if I startled you earlier this evening.'

'You mean by jumping out of the shadows while I'm standing by a recently dead body lying in a pool of blood?' Benny shrugged. 'Think nothing of it. Silly of me to get a bit apprehensive when a cold-blooded murderer leaps out at me. Can I go now?' she asked. 'I mean if you just brought me here to apologise. Or was there something else?' She smiled innocently.

Luci seemed puzzled. 'Of course you can go,' she said.

'I can?' Benny asked in amazement.

'Well, yes.' Luci seemed suddenly scandalized. 'You're not a prisoner here,' she said.

'I'm so sorry.' Benny stood up and opened her arms to take in the room. 'I thought this was a cell.' She made a point of looking round, nodding and tutting as if checking out a hotel room. 'How many stars does this place get in *Where to Stay in Picturesque Kasagrad*?'

As she spoke, the door opened again and Herv Gresham stepped into the room. He closed the door firmly behind him.

'Or should that be picaresque?' Benny wondered out loud

as she watched him.

Gresham seemed amused by the comment. He took his time walking to the table, and perched on the edge, watching Benny. 'I'm not sure that we are all quite the rogues you seem to think,' he told her.

'I seem to keep apologising,' Benny replied. 'But, can I point out again that I've been dragged from my hotel room...' She paused. 'Okay, so hotel room is maybe a bit rich, but it was rather more homely that the accommodation you're apparently offering.'

Gresham was still amused. 'This is a cell,' he said simply.

'Ah!' Benny pointed accusingly at Luci Yendipp. 'You see? I told you this was a cell. Hah!' she quipped. 'You can't keep me fooled for long.'

'In that case,' Luci said, also amused now, 'you will have realized two other things.'

'Oh? Surprise me.'

'First, that I have been trying extremely hard not to kill you, or allow you to come to harm.'

Benny sighed. 'Must have missed that one.'

'And second, that this is the lowest level of the citadel.'

'Yeah,' Benny conceded. 'I did get that.'

'And that the room is constructed from hematite. The door is lead clad in oak, braced with steel.'

'Absolutely.' Benny nodded. 'Is it?'

'In short,' Gresham said, 'this is the one room in the citadel where we can talk in safety. In the knowledge that the Fifth Axis listening devices trained on us from their barracks won't pick up the sound of our breath as we whisper what we really think about them. It's the one place in this building, possibly on this planet, where we can talk.'

Benny did not take her eyes from his solemn face as she pulled the chair out and sat down again. 'So, talk,' she said levelly.

Bryn Lavers was sneaking out of the side door when they picked him up. He was still wearing the waiter disguise under a long coat. He had slipped the face plate off and stuffed it in his coat pocket. The ground car barely paused for long enough to get the door open, Lavers inside, and the door closed again. Then it was rejoining the highway.

Lavers's first thought was that it was the militia come to get him. He was only slightly relieved to see Kendrick's half-face leering at him across the back seat of the car.

'You did imply it was important,' Kendrick said with an ill-disguised sneer. 'I don't need to point out to you that it better had be.'

Lavers swallowed. 'Of course. Yes. I, er – well.'

'Yes?'

He took a deep breath and his words followed it in a rush. 'You asked me to keep an eye on Professor Summerfield. They picked her up tonight. Took her away.'

'Who picked her up?' Kendrick demanded.

'Militia. Government types.'

'Sure?'

Lavers shrugged. 'Gresham was with them.'

A dark figure swung round in the front seat to face them. The man's face emerged into the light, and Lavers shrank back as he saw it was Kendrick's adjutant. 'That means she's important to them,' the man said. 'Do you think they know?'

Kendrick snorted. 'What could they know?' He sat back, relaxing slightly. 'It's more likely a reaction to the death of Ilsa Devereux. They know Summerfield made contact with her.'

'That's possible,' the adjutant agreed.

'Death?' Lavers said, his voice hoarse. 'She's dead?'

'She met with an unfortunate accident this evening,' Kendrick said with evident satisfaction.

'She met with a sharp knife this evening,' the adjutant added.

Lavers slumped back in his seat. He looked out of the window. But the toughened glass was darkly tinted and he could see nothing save his own reflection, his own shame staring back at him.

* * *

They talked for a long time. Soon after they started, a militia man came into the room and there was a pause as he spoke quietly to Gresham.

'They know you're here,' Gresham said to Benny when the man had gone.

'Who do?'

'The Fifth Axis. Kendrick.'

'And how do you know that?' Benny asked him.

He smiled. 'We have ways and means,' he assured her.

Then Luci continued with her story. She explained how she had found her brother's body in the hallway after Benny and Straklant left. She smiled thinly at Benny's shock, and told her she had no doubt that Benny knew nothing about it. She explained how she had followed them to Hennessy's, how she had wanted nothing more than to find and kill Straklant.

Benny, for her part, told Luci of Straklant's death in the escape pod.

Luci, it seemed, had managed to get down to Kasagrad, and then made contact with Gresham, whom she knew by repute.

'I was happy to help,' Gresham explained. 'Straklant was stationed here, as Kendrick's number two. So we knew all about him. He led the division that massacred the inhabitants on Frastus Minima,' he said, glancing at Luci. She looked away, biting her lower lip. 'A nasty piece of work, even by Fifth Axis standards.'

'So what happens now?' Benny asked. 'Straklant is dead, so why did you want to see me?'

'Because we need your help,' Gresham said.

'Mine? Hey, I'm new here. I don't even know who's on which side yet.'

Gresham smiled again, a humourless, thin smile. 'You can be here for a long time and still not know that,' he said. 'But Straklant came to you. He wanted your help to find the Tomb of Rablev. He believed that you could do it. That's why we need your help.'

'To find a lost tomb?' Benny gave a short laugh. 'Why?'

Gresham laughed as well, with equal lack of humour. 'I have no idea,' he said. 'But I want to find it before Kendrick and the Fifth Axis do. It's obviously important to them, and that can't be for any reason that's good news to us.'

'But it's just a legend.'

'It's a legend,' Gresham said, 'which persuaded Raul Kendrick to send his best officer to Braxiatel to get you. They believed you could find the tomb. I don't know if you can or not, but I hope you can at least tell me why they're so desperate to find it.'

Benny considered this. 'You must have some idea yourself,' she said. 'Straklant gave us a story about historical interest and preserving art and archaeology treasures. I'd guess from what you've both told me that this wasn't his most pressing concern.'

'Straklant was a Philistine,' Luci said. 'He wouldn't know an art treasure if it fell on his head. And if it did, he'd blow holes in it for good measure.'

'Only one thing matters to Kendrick, and that's complete control of Kasagrad.'

Benny looked Gresham in the eye. 'Some people feel that he already has that,' she said, 'in everything but name.'

There was a sadness in his eyes. 'I'm afraid that isn't as far from the truth as we would like. But there are pragmatics involved here. Considerations that don't seem to have occurred to the late Ilsa Deveraux and her compatriots.'

'Late?' Benny frowned.

'She was dumped in an alley behind her flat with her throat slit,' Luci said.

Benny shook her head in sadness and disbelief. 'And you say Kendrick's not in charge here?'

'If he were in charge it would have been a public execution.' Gresham stood up from the table. 'Let me tell you how it is,' he said. 'Honestly how it is.'

'Okay.'

'We're an embarrassment and an annoyance to the Axis

forces in general and to the Imperator in particular. They control everything in this sector – directly control it. Except us. And while we're still free to an extent behind their front line, that compromises their advance.'

'So why don't they just invade?' Benny asked.

'They would. In fact, our intelligence tells us that they will. We know we can't hold out against them, but we can give them grief, slow down their other advances for as long as possible. While we hold out.'

Benny began to see what he was saying. 'So you co-operate just enough to delay the invasion.'

Gresham nodded. 'They know that as things stand they'll take huge losses if they try a direct invasion. This citadel, for all its insecurities, enables us to keep control of the minefields and smartbombs that encircle the planet. They can blockade us, they can cut us off from the rest of the galaxy, but they can't get in here and turn off the defences.'

'They can overwhelm the planet by sheer force of numbers,' Luci said, 'but not without making a massive commitment of troops from elsewhere and not without losing many of them.'

'But there will come a point where we can offer no more concessions,' Gresham said. 'At the moment, arguably, we're better off as we are than if the Axis were in direct control. It's a dubious benefit I know, but they still have to resort to murder and assassination rather than just shooting dissenters on the street. But they're getting impatient.' He sighed. 'The invasion will come. They know it and we know it. So now they're looking for ways to reduce their losses. They are also,' he said meaningfully, 'looking for the Lost Tomb of Rablev. Now, I can't imagine how that fits with their main objective but I am sure that it does. But,' he went on, 'if anyone can imagine what the connection is, I think it's you.'

Benny considered this. 'I'll need a day or two,' she said.

'A day or two may be all we have,' Gresham said. 'I told you that it was a good thing they have to resort to murder. But that doesn't make it acceptable.'

'What can you do about it?'

'I can recommend to the Concordance that we use it as the excuse we need to expel the Fifth Axis forces from this planet.'

'Isn't that pushing it a bit?'

'We can't afford to have them still here when they start their invasion,' Gresham said. He smiled. 'That would make it far too easy. We've always known that when the invasion is imminent, we have to expel them. We thought about just locking them all up, but we really don't have the facilities and we can't spare the troops to keep an eye on them.'

'Why not use them as hostages?' Luci asked. 'It's what they'd do. If the invasion goes ahead, you execute them.'

Gresham seemed irritated by the suggestion. 'Firstly, because I doubt they'd care,' he said. 'And secondly, because it's what they'd do. If we are willing to stoop to their methods and philosophy, we might as well give up now. No,' he went on quickly as if to dispel the subject, 'the problem will be managing the propaganda of cause and effect. We don't want the people thinking that the Axis are attacking because of our actions. This way, we have a legal and a political justification.'

'Neat,' Benny agreed. 'With just one small caveat, of course.'

'Of course,' Gresham said. 'We'd all rather have an excuse that didn't include a young woman lying dead in the gutter.'

There was silence for almost a minute. Then Benny said: 'So, let me see if I've got this straight. You're going to throw out Kendrick and his cohorts, and they're going to try to invade. So you want me to find out how they think this lost tomb thing can help them. Right?'

'Pretty much.'

'And what else can I do to help?' Benny asked. 'I mean, in my spare time?'

Gresham and Luci both looked at her with a seriousness that led Benny to suspect they were not big on sarcasm.

'The only way we could actually repel the attack,' Gresham

said slowly, 'is if we know their command frequency for the operation. Get us that, and we can hold them off. Maybe even inflict enough damage that they're forced to abandon this sector.'

'Oh, right.' Benny waved her hand in the air. 'Well, why didn't you say so before? What is a command frequency, by the way? Just out of interest, you understand.'

'The whole operation will be computerised. The Fifth Axis Command and Control structure assumes that whatever codes and encryption they use will be broken by the enemy.'

'Very wise, judging by history,' Benny said.

'So to stop the enemy intercepting the orders and reacting, they not only encrypt them but they broadcast simultaneously on hundreds of different frequencies.'

'And how does that help?'

'They broadcast different sets of orders and instructions on each frequency. The computer systems generate dummy instructions designed to mislead the enemy. Only one set is genuine – those on the command frequency. And that changes every day. It is known only to the commanders in the field.'

'The end result,' Luci said, 'is that it's better to ignore it all than try to guess what they're up to from the comms traffic.'

'Right.' Benny blew a long breath upwards from her mouth so that her fringe shuddered in the breeze. 'So all you want me to do is solve the riddle of the lost tomb, find out what they're up to, and discover what super-secret frequency they're using to plan the invasion.'

'Yes,' Gresham agreed. 'That's all.'

Understandably, Benny's first decision was that she needed a drink. She had pretty much abandoned the hope of any sleep for the foreseeable future, but a good stiff drink at Piccolini's and a word with Georgia the Forger seemed like the next best thing.

Her priorities changed as soon as she got to the bar. Piccolini came across to her, the room was almost empty. He was open all night, but towards morning even the late drinkers drifted away or keeled over and were dragged outside to the pavement.

'Georgia went home,' Piccolini told her. 'She said to say she's taken the data with her, whatever that means. I was wondering when we'd see you again,' he added. It was as close as Benny had heard from him to an expression of real concern.

'I'm fine,' she told him. 'Some people down town just wanted a chat, that's all. Don't worry about it.'

'If you're sure,' he told her, producing a bottle. 'And if you're up to it, your friend is in.'

'My friend?'

'Mikey.' He pointed across to a table on the other side of the room. 'With the moustache. You were asking.'

'Yes,' Benny said. But her voice seemed filtered through water. 'Yes, I was.' Almost in a dream she cautiously made her way across the bar to the table where the large man sat.

His head was down, an empty bottle on the table in front of him. But even angled as it was, Benny could see his huge moustache bristling. As she reached the table and sat down opposite the man, he snored loudly.

'Mikey?' she asked hesitantly. Then, when there was no reaction, louder: 'Mikey!'

He snorted awake, disorientated for a moment, catching sight of Benny and trying to focus. 'Who wants to know?' he asked, rubbing his eyes. He stopped rubbing in surprise and disappointment as he caught sight of the empty bottle.

Benny handed him her full bottle of beer.

'Thanks,' he said. 'Yeah, I'm Mikey. What do you want?'

'I want to know,' she told him, 'how you came to get your photo taken four hundred years ago.'

He frowned, thinking. 'Yeah. Right. It was down on the Baxenplass. This guy came up with a camera. Old-fashioned thing. Even had a film,' he added with a measure of contempt.

Benny watched him closely. How long had this man lived,

she wondered. Come to that, how did he remember back that far. 'Not that photograph,' she said gently, hoping she wasn't about to shatter his fragile memory. 'This was outside a tomb. There was a man –' she started to go on.

'That's right.' He nodded with muted enthusiasm. 'Fifth Axis guy. Said he wanted local colour.'

'No, no.' Benny tied to make eye contact. His eyes, she saw, were red with drink and lack of sleep and she wondered for a moment how her own eyes looked to him. 'This was four hundred years ago.'

He stared at her. 'Four weeks,' he said eventually. 'I think. Might have been five.' He swigged the beer. 'Not hundreds of years ago,' he slurred round the bottle. Then he struggled to his feet and stood proudly by the wall behind the table, striking the exact same pose that Benny knew so well. Only this time he was not torn in half down the middle. 'Stood like this,' he said. 'Just the other week. Not years – hundreds of years ago. That would be ridico–' He paused, concentrating, and tried again: 'ridolocus.'

'Ridiculous,' Benny said quietly. 'That's what I thought.' She stood up and reached out to shake his hand.

For a moment he thought she wanted the bottle back, and curled away from her, protecting it with his body. Benny dropped her hand, let it go. 'Thanks,' she said softly. 'Excuse me, but I have to talk to someone about a forged photograph. A whole forged document in fact.' Suddenly some things at least were becoming clearer.

But others were receding into the haze of confusion.

Georgia's reaction to Benny's breathless: 'The photo's a fake' was less than impressive as far as Benny was concerned.

'Well, a lot of this is a fake,' she said. 'And to be strictly accurate, if you mean this photograph,' she went on as she displayed it on the screen, 'then actually only parts of it are faked.'

'Oh,' Benny said, more than slightly crestfallen. 'You knew that already.'

Georgia was working in a small room at the back of her tiny house which she called the 'studio.' There was barely room for both of them to squeeze in. Georgia had sent the children to a neighbour's before she went with Benny to Piccolini's and had been hard at work on the manuscript since she returned.

'I mean,' she said, bristling with professional disdain, 'look at this guy at the back here.'

Benny looked. It was Jason, leaning in the shadows. 'What about him?'

'Well just that it's such a poor job. Talk about botched.' She leaned forward to point at the screen, at the same time magnifying the image to show what she was talking about. 'Look at the way the light source changes, the direction of the shadows is just completely wrong. Then there's the contrast, way too high.' She shook her head and clicked her tongue. 'It's just such a mess. Jaggies all over the place. A kid with a blunt pocketknife might have done it. Anyone can spot it as a fake a mile off.'

'Absolutely,' Benny agreed with a casual laugh. 'Anyone. I wasn't fooled,' she added quickly. 'Not for a moment, not me. Hah!'

'It just makes a mockery of the care and attention that I put into the rest of it,' Georgia went on. 'Mikey's all right. Not perfect by any means, but he fits right in. At least the tear looks genuine, it's no joke trying to match an uneven edge like that believe you me.'

'I'm sure,' Benny agreed, still staring at Jason and trying to see what Georgia meant about the shadows and the light source. Then her brain caught up with her ears. 'Do you mean you faked this?' she demanded.

'Well, obviously not Mr Jaggie at the back there.'

'Jason,' Benny murmured.

'Whoever. They came to me because I'm the best, but then they go and botch it. They wanted me to leave a gap to matte him into. Didn't have the source image when I was working on it. That was something they needed to get from

165

somewhere else and add later.' She shook her head again. 'It's so annoying, I mean I know it was a rush job, but I told them exactly what to do.'

'Annoying,' Benny agreed, 'is the word. If it's any consolation,' she added sadly, 'the original wasn't really up to much.'

'The original image, you mean?'

'Well,' Benny said, 'that too.' She sighed, pushing thoughts of Jason to the back of her mind with a supreme effort. 'So, how much of this document did you actually fake?' she asked.

'Bits and pieces,' Georgia admitted. 'They really just wanted local colour from me. That's what Straklant said, anyway.'

'Straklant?'

'I think that was his name, yes. Fifth Axis. Paid well, though. Tall man, slim, blond. Charming.'

'That was him,' Benny agreed.

'But there's far more been added in here than just what I did.'

'So,' Benny said glumly, 'it's all a fake.'

'Oh no.' Georgia was surprised at Benny's comment. 'Most of it is quite genuine. About ten per cent is new material. And Lacey's manuscript, what we can recover of it from the video footage, that's all genuine of course. In fact, it's by matching to that we can tell what's covering up Goram's half.'

'Covering up?' Benny's head was swimming with a mixture of bewilderment, disappointment and tiredness.

'Well, it was done for a reason,' Georgia pointed out. 'And what's been added is mostly pretty anodyne. Blank pages even in some cases.'

'So,' Benny said slowly, 'if it wasn't put in there to add new stuff, it was put in to cover up, to eliminate what was there before.'

'Exactly.' Georgia smiled, like a teacher to a bright pupil who's just catching on. 'Harder to spot that way than if you just excise material. That would leave a data trace. To say nothing of the rogue end of file markers creeping in where they shouldn't, skipping data tracks, everything.' She turned her attention back to the screen. 'I wonder why they did it.'

'Well they added Jason to get me hooked,' Benny said. 'And they got me hooked to get hold of Lacey's half of the manuscript. But what they're covering up, I don't know.' She yawned. 'I think I'll sleep on it,' she said through the yawn.

'Mmmm,' Georgia said. But she was already fully immersed in lining up images on the screen. 'See you then.'

Benny was almost asleep on her feet by the time she got to her room at Piccolini's.

So it wasn't much of a leap to assume she was dreaming when she pushed open the door and saw who was sitting on the side of the bed waiting for her.

'Hello, Benny. How nice to renew your acquaintance.'

But something in his voice told her she was wide awake. Then she saw the gun he was holding. And Kolonel Daglan Straklant, personal adjutant to Marshal Raul Kendrick, rose slowly to his feet and smiled. He raised the gun. 'However briefly.'

10
Pieced Together

'Do you want a drink?' Benny went over to the small dressing table, aware that the gun was tracking her movement. 'I think I need one.' There was a half empty bottle of wine in amongst the bits and pieces. She hunted round for a glass.

'Not while I'm working, thank you,' Straklant said. He seemed amused at Benny's feigned nonchalance. Amused, but not deceived.

'So,' Benny said as she poured, trying to keep her hand steady. 'The old escape pod ruse, eh? Your friends get you out, then blow it up and make sure everyone thinks you're dead.' She swallowed a mouthful of acidic wine with an effort. 'It's one of the oldest tricks in the book,' she said.

'It's one of the most effective,' he retorted.

'But why bother?' Benny swept a pile of clothes from the grubby stool by the dressing table and sat down. 'I mean, you had the manuscript from Hennessy and you must have expected me to be dead.'

'I like to cover all eventualities.'

'And is that why you're here? Covering your eventualities?'

'I came to recover Goram's half of the manuscript.' He waved the gun, gesturing at the room in general. 'Since it isn't here, I assume it's in your rucksack.' The gun ended up pointing at the rucksack at Benny's feet.

'You assume wrong,' she said. 'But why do you want to bother with me? I was only useful to you in locating Lacey's half of the manuscript. Why do you want the other half back?' She leaned forward, watching him closely, hoping for a reaction. 'We both know it's a forgery,' she said. 'Or at least, partly faked, as a way of getting me involved.' But he didn't even blink. 'So why do you want it back? You have the only copy of Lacey's half, so what are you afraid I might discover from what you've left me of Goram's?'

'It's evidence,' he said. 'And any evidence is a little too much. Just as any witness is one too many.'

Benny tried to sound at ease, amused even. 'Ah, well, you're too late then. We all know you want to get into the Tomb.'

'That's what Gresham told you, is it?' He smiled as she started. 'Oh, we know you've been to see him. Just as we know that he can't begin to guess what our plans are.'

'Your plans are to invade,' Benny shot back angrily. 'To subjugate another innocent world and suppress its people.'

He shrugged. 'Of course. But that's not as bad as you seem to think.'

'Hah!'

'You say "innocent", but you've seen what it's like down there in the bar. There are fights every night. Drunken slobs who haven't done a decent day's work for years, no discipline, no productivity, no pride.' Straklant leaned forward, his eyes glittering as they caught the light from the bare bulb above. 'We can give them something to live for. Something to feel proud of and be a part of. We can make them feel they're doing something, achieving something. Working to the greater good of everyone.'

'What about Ilsa?' Benny said bitterly. Her bitterness was partly from the shame that she could not even remember the woman's surname. 'She had pride, she achieved, she was part of something. A young woman with hopes and aspirations. What about her?'

He was dismissive. 'There are always some people who don't fit in, who are selfish enough to work against the greater good for their own gratification and glory. She had her moment of fame, that's really all she wanted.'

'I doubt it,' Benny said angrily. She stood up, slamming her glass down on the table. 'I can't believe she wanted to end up dead in the gutter. Probably all she really aspired to was a peaceful life, a good job, a few real friendships, a loving husband and a real home.' Her voice cracked slightly.

Benny felt her knees trembling and she sat down again.

'Well,' Straklant said as he stood up. 'We'll never know, will we?' He gestured with the gun. 'Get up, it's time to go.'

'Go?'

'I believe you,' he said shortly. 'So, let's go.'

'You believe me? You mean, you agree that invading this planet will –'

He cut her off with a short laugh. 'I mean I believe that the manuscript isn't in your rucksack. So I think we'll go somewhere with a little more privacy, and discuss for as long as it takes where it really is.' His smile was a curl of the thin lips. 'Don't disappoint me,' he said quietly, a cruel edge in his voice. 'I'm hoping our discussion will take some time.'

Straklant stepped forward, holding the gun close to Benny's head.

She stepped back, pushing his hand away sharply. 'Never – ever – raise your hands to a lady,' she snapped angrily. Before he could respond, she raised her own hands above her shoulders and turned to the door.

It was an old trick, but Benny had to admire the gall with which Straklant pulled it off. He draped his coat over his arm so that it covered the gun. The end of the barrel was just visible beneath if you looked closely. But nobody other than Benny would look closely. He held her arm firmly in his free hand – the false hand, Benny remembered. Probably all the stronger for it, unfortunately.

Benny looked for Piccolini as they crossed the bar. But he was nowhere to be seen. In fact, she could see nobody she recognised. No sign even of Mikey. No way of escape.

As they approached the door it swung open violently and a man walked in. It was the young man who had sat with Ilsa. His face was older today, lined with lack of sleep and grief. His eyes glistened with suppressed tears. He was walking fast, determined as he came in, narrowly avoiding a collision with one of the blank-faced waiters who was standing just inside the door. Almost immediately he caught sight of Benny, and then of Straklant behind her.

And Straklant's uniform.

Benny could see what was happening before it occurred to Straklant that there was a problem, and she braced herself, ready to pull free. The man launched himself towards Straklant, not caring that Benny was between them.

'You murdering –' he screamed as he flew through the air. The end of what he was saying was lost in Benny's shout, Straklant's cry of annoyance as she pulled away, and the crash of the table that the two men landed on as it collapsed.

Benny's arm was sore, but she was free of him. Her first thought was to run. But she could hear the sounds of the struggle behind her, and turned. The man was on top of Straklant, his fist raised to thump him. Hard.

But then Straklant's own hand came up. Benny shouted a warning as the coat slid away and the gun was revealed. The man saw it as Benny shouted, and adjusted his aim, punching instead at the gun. His fist connected as Straklant fired. The blast of energy went wide, slamming into the ceiling and making the lights shake as plaster fell to the floor. The gun was flying across the room, skidding across the floor.

Straklant's other hand, his left hand, came up. But it was not aiming a punch at the man astride him. He seemed instead to be reaching into his own mouth. And as Benny watched, his teeth clamped down on his index finger, biting hard as he pulled the hand away again.

To reveal a long spike protruding from the stumpy knuckle. The metal flashed in the swaying light as Straklant lunged forwards. It was almost silent. The sounds of conversation and drinking in the bar had already stopped. The piano stilled. The young man did not even have time to cry out as the blade lanced into his eye. For a moment they were absolutely still: the young man poised above Straklant ready to thump him again, fist raised; Straklant reaching up to him.

Slowly, the man sagged. His arm dropped to his side, and he toppled slowly backwards. At that moment, Straklant pulled out the blade, with the same sudden force as he had plunged it in. A gush of blood and clear viscous liquid streamed out after it, staining Straklant's jacket as he pushed the dead weight of the body away and struggled to his feet.

By which time Piccolini was shouting across the bar, and Benny was running for the door.

Only the waiter stood between her and escape. The robot hesitated, as if unsure which way to move. Benny thrust it aside as she passed. Or tried to pass. Suddenly the robot was holding her tight, pressing her arms to her side and turning her back to face Straklant.

'Hold her, Lavers,' Straklant barked as he approached. 'This isn't finished yet. Not by a long way.' He stepped over the supine body of the young man without seeming to notice it. Absently he brushed down the bloodied front of his jacket with his good hand. The spiked finger of his other hand was raised ready as he approached. It was dripping.

'I'm sorry.' The voice was a faint whimper close to Benny's ear. Bizarrely it seemed to come from inside the waiter's head.

'So am I,' she said automatically. She tried to turn, tried to pull free. 'But what's one more death after so many?' she said quietly. 'And there will be thousands more before long. We'll probably never know how many.'

The arms holding her weakened their grip slightly. 'So many,' the quiet voice whispered. 'What have we done?' it sobbed. 'What are we doing?' And the waiter let go of her. It stepped to one side, head hanging as if it were looking at the floor, at the trickle of blood that was running towards to door. Running after Benny.

'Lavers!' Straklant shouted as the door slammed shut behind Benny. The waiter did not move.

Straklant hesitated only a moment. He could chase after Benny, but the chances were that he had lost her already.

And she had been right, apart from the amusement and closure that it would give, she really was not important any more. He took a step towards the door. The waiter moved across, as if to block him.

'This has gone too far.' Even filtered by the face plate, Lavers's voice was nervous, hesitant. 'Let her go.'

Ignoring the people now clustered round the bleeding body on the floor behind him, Straklant beckoned over another of the robot waiters. 'I think your colleague,' he said slowly, nodding towards the metallic figure standing in front of the door, 'is malfunctioning.'

The robot waiter swung slowly round to look.

'He seems to think he is not a robot at all, but human.'

'Damn you, Straklant,' the voice hissed. 'Of course I'm human. You know I'm human.' A pause, then with a little more confidence, Lavers added: 'More human than you.'

'You see what I mean?' Straklant's voice was almost oily with false sympathy. He clicked his tongue and shook his head. 'Most unfortunate. I doubt it can be repaired. You just can't get the parts these days, can you.'

He watched as Lavers struggled with the tiny nuts at the back of the faceplate. He seemed to be having trouble with them. Straklant could guess how his sweating fingers were slipping inside the bulky gloves, unable to gain a purchase on the tight screw heads. 'I suggest you disassemble the thing.'

'What?' There was panic in Lavers voice now. Fear as the waiter closed on him, followed by another. 'Stop, I am human!' They had his arms now, were stretching them out from his body, applying pressure at the socket joints.

Straklant stepped past them. 'It's obviously a deep-rooted problem,' he said calmly as he opened the door. He spared a single backward glance, smiling in satisfaction as another of the robots took hold of Lavers's bullet-like head and started to twist.

'Reuse what you can, won't you,' Straklant said as he let the door swing shut behind him. But his words were lost in the screams from Lavers, and the shouts of the customers.

'Switch it off.'

Gresham had cracked first. He sat grey-faced and sickened in the basement cell of the Citadel. Luci Yendipp turned off the transmitter, and the confused sounds of pain and panic were cut off.

'Well, least we know that Benny got away from him,' she said.

'We hope she did,' Gresham corrected her. 'From the sound of it that's two more murdered at least.' He sighed. 'More than enough to go with. Maybe enough to persuade them we should indict Straklant.'

'I told you he wasn't dead,' Luci said. There was no hint of pride or conceit in her voice. Just fact. 'I think we may need more help.'

'Poor Lavers,' Gresham said quietly. 'He really didn't have a clue, did he?'

'What will they do when they find the transmitter inside the headpiece?'

Gresham shrugged. 'I doubt they'll notice it. Lavers didn't and it's been there long enough. They'll have...' He swallowed. '...Other things on their minds, I imagine.' He shook his head and leaned forward, rubbing at his temples with his fingers. His head felt like it was about to burst. 'What sort of help were you thinking of?' he asked.

'Well,' Luci said, 'it was just an idea, but since Professor Summerfield is very definitely involved...'

Benny was both more calm and more determined when she arrived at Georgia's. She had spent some time and effort in making sure she had not been followed. The last thing she wanted was to lead Straklant or any of his associates to Georgia.

'I thought you were getting some sleep,' Georgia remarked when she opened the door.

'Slight change of plan,' Benny said and explained what

175

had happened. 'I think things are getting rather more urgent on both sides,' she said as they squeezed themselves back into the small studio.

'Let me show you what I've managed to put together so far,' Georgia said. She angled the screen so they could both see. 'Oh, and you can have your ball back,' she added, tossing Joseph across to Benny. 'I've copied the data on to my own server.'

'Thanks.' She stuffed him into her rucksack.

As Georgia paged through the reconstructed manuscript, she gave Benny a running commentary. At each page, she explained what she had been able to do, and then they both read it carefully. Some pages were still missing on the Lacey side. Some were just plain illegible due to the lack of a decent picture on Joseph's video material. And several of the pages in the Goram side of the manuscript were crossed through in red.

'I've indicated where believe the material has been added,' Georgia said. 'Either I know it's a fake because I did some of it, or because it doesn't match what's on the other side. There are also some pages that I just think look suspicious. I've marked them too, but we've probably missed a few, even so.'

'Never mind,' Benny said. 'This is excellent. Well done.' She examined a page of hand-drawn diagrams with a red line through them.

'I just don't understand why they'd want you to think this stuff was genuine,' Georgia said. 'What did they think you would infer from that?' She jabbed a finger at the screen.

'I don't know,' Benny admitted. 'The photo was faked to get me involved. They needed me to lead them to the Lacey half, and I did that all right.' She gestured for Georgia to move on and another page appeared. This time the two halves matched. There was handwritten text, most if it readable despite a few smudges and an area that had been damaged by damp at some point. In the margin were several small line-drawings.

'What's this mean, do you suppose?' Georgia asked pointing to one of the drawings. 'It crops up several times. There's an account later of them reaching some sort of inner sanctum of the tomb, and it's all over that page.'

Benny shrugged. The sketch was a simple circular design, segments alternatively shaded and empty. 'It looks like...' She frowned. What did it look like? 'It looks like a spool of tape,' she realised. She considered this. 'A tape... Maybe they recorded something. A video tape even?'

'Maybe it will tell us later on,' Georgia said.

'It might explain why Straklant was anxious,' Benny mused. 'If the symbol crops up on the half he knows we have then it might clue us in that there's more evidence around.' She sucked air through her teeth. 'Somewhere.' She turned her attention to the text.

'It's interesting, isn't it?' Georgia remarked as Benny read. 'This part of the planet used to be desert. The Citadel has been here for ever, pretty much. It was a monument of some sort. But the community round it is comparatively recent. Just a thousand or so years old in fact.' She smiled at Benny. 'I did some reading while you were gone.'

'I can see why.' Benny whistled softly. 'The tomb,' she murmured. 'It's here.'

'Somewhere here,' Georgia agreed. She pointed to a paragraph. 'They were actually doing a survey of the Citadel, trying to discover how old it is, digging down to the foundations.'

'And they fell through.' Benny read aloud from the screen: 'My shovel pitched through the sand, and I almost fell into the darkness that was revealed beneath. I had punctured a thin membrane of some sort, cloth perhaps, that was covering the area round the entrance. I called to Goram to bring a lamp and he joined me.' Benny considered. 'I wonder if Straklant and his lot knew that,' she said. 'They do now, of course, but did they when they first came to me?'

'Is it important?' Georgia asked.

'The one thing the Fifth Axis is desperate for is a way to

disable the defence grid controlled from the Citadel,' Benny told her. 'Now we discover that the Lost Tomb of Rablev – which we know they are looking for – is somewhere very close to it. Maybe even joined to it.' She nodded. 'Oh yes. It's important.'

The next page was again half ruled through with red. But the faked half of the page was blank.

'I think they were just bored with this one,' Georgia said. She went to move on.

'No, wait,' Benny told her. She was looking at the fuzzy image on the other side of the page, copied across from the video of Lacey's half of the manuscript. 'Can you make that any clearer?'

Georgia thought about it. 'Possibly. If you think it's worth the effort.'

Benny leaned back. 'I think it's worth the effort,' she said. 'We're both tired. We've been missing the point.'

'The point being?'

'That the photo of Jason was the exception. That was the only thing they actually put in there for us to find.' Benny looked at her. 'Don't you see? This is just a blank page. It isn't what they've added that should be of interest. It's what they're covering up.'

'What they don't want us to see,' Georgia realised.

Benny nodded. 'There's two things we need,' she said with renewed determination. 'We need to look closely at everything on the other side of the page from our red-liners.'

'Agreed. And the other thing?'

'Coffee,' Benny said. 'An awful lot of coffee.'

'So now we know.'

Benny and Georgia both sat staring at the screen.

'Yes,' Georgia said quietly.

'How long does it take to arrange an invasion, do you suppose?' Benny wondered. 'Because Straklant has had both halves for a while now. He knows what we know. In fact, he's always known. That's why they wanted the other half.'

'The only thing they didn't know was exactly where the tomb is,' Georgia agreed.

'And they could hardly go digging up every street and house round the Citadel without at least attracting some attention.' Benny bit on the end of a fingernail as she thought it through. 'In fact,' she said, 'we're probably about at the point they were at when they started. Which doesn't bode too well.'

Ironically, it had been on the opposite side of the page to the faked photograph of Mikey and Jason that they found what they were looking for. It was a diagram of the internal structure of the tomb.

'What are these?' Georgia had asked. 'They come up from every room except this one.'

Some reading up on the legends and beliefs of the time in amongst some of the handwritten notes that accompanied the diagram offered the answer.

'I've come across similar beliefs,' Benny said as she explained. 'The notion is that the soul of the dead person departs from their body and ascends to the stars, to the heavens. Through these.' She traced her finger along the double line that ran upwards from one of the burial chambers. It was cut off at the ragged edge of the inserted photograph.

'This room doesn't have any,' Georgia pointed out. 'Yet they've drawn a coffin there.'

Benny squinted. 'Rablev,' she said. 'I guess his punishment was that his soul was trapped here for ever. No vent, so no ascension and no happy afterlife and serve him right.'

They had been about to turn the page, when Benny spotted something else. 'Is that on the video?' she asked. 'Or is it really part of the drawing?' It was a line cutting diagonally down the page. If it continued then most of it would be on the facing page, replaced by the photograph.

Georgia assured her it was a part of the diagram, and Benny looked again, closer this time. 'It's a distinctive shape. Some form of structure over the top of the tomb. Like the way they depicted the Citadel earlier, remember?' Her blood froze as she said it. 'Of course, the Citadel.'

Benny was on her feet, rummaging through the things on Georgia's desk. Eventually she found a ruler and slapped it across the screen.

'What are you doing?'

'These vents all point at the same star constellation, at the same point, right?'

'If you say so.'

'I say so. And we know from the notes we've read that there's another chamber that is off to the left, underneath where the photo now is.'

'Yes. So?'

'So...' She paused. 'You know, there's something familiar about the whole shape of this tomb, if only I could work out what it is. Long and thin, with a central passageway and chambers off, then a single small chamber at the end of the passage...' Benny shook her head and moved the ruler across the screen, keeping it angled to match the vents. 'Anyway, that can wait. Now, if that other chamber were about here...' She stopped and considered. 'Which it would be, so as to give the symmetry with the other side of the central passageway...'

'Then the vents from it,' Georgia said slowly as she worked it out, 'would pass...' She halted, her finger running up the ruler to the point where it would have cut into the diagonal line if the photo were not in the way.

'They'd pass,' Benny said, 'right through the lower level of the Citadel. Now,' she went on, 'we haven't found anything yet that tells us how big they are.'

'They look pretty big on the diagram.'

'And they're probably blocked up at the top end. Though only by a few bricks and a bit of mortar, I suspect.'

'In which case, someone who knew they were there, and could get into the tomb...'

'Could climb up, break through into the Citadel at some point, though we don't know where,' Benny said, 'and disable the defence grid.' Benny and Georgia were staring at each other solemnly now. 'Leaving the way open for Kendrick and Straklant to bring in their invasion force without any resistance at all. Do you have any brandy?'

Georgia was considering the implications of this. 'I'll get it,' she said.

11
Doomsday

There was only enough brandy for two small glasses. After it was gone, they allowed themselves just one more cup of coffee. Then Benny said: 'We should get going. We need to tell Gresham what's going on.'

Georgia had been quiet, thoughtful, as they sat and drank. Now she looked up and Benny could see that there was a depth of sadness in her eyes. 'I'm not coming,' she said.

'What?'

'Sorry.'

Benny was confused. 'But, this is your world. And we worked this out together. I still need your help,' she went on. 'I don't know where the tomb actually is. I don't really know the city, come to that. Your planet is about to be invaded – don't you care about that?' It was a cheap shot, and she knew it. But she was so surprised and annoyed that she could not help herself.

'I'm sorry,' Georgia said. 'But that's just it. Of course I care.' She took Benny's arm, drew her slightly closer. 'Do what you can,' she said. 'Please. But my place is here. With my children.'

'We can prevent this,' Benny said quietly. 'If you help me, I think –'

'That's just it though. You only think you can. And we both know that probably you can't.' There were tears in her eyes now. 'This is my world, you're right. But this is my home. My family. I owe it to them to be here when...' She looked away, her voice catching. 'When it happens.'

'But don't you at least want to try to stop it?'

'Stop it?' She laughed. 'We can't stop it. It'll be a bloodbath. We all know about Frastus, and the others. Benny,' she said, 'this is our darkest hour. Maybe our last hour. And I owe it to my children to be with them, to help them all I can. They have no father, not any more. I'm all they've got. I need to be here for them. Please don't begrudge me that.'

'I don't begrudge you anything,' Benny said. She was almost crying herself now, biting her lip, blinking away the tears. 'Of course I don't.'

'It's all right for you,' Georgia said. 'You don't have children or a family to worry about.'

Benny stood up, grabbed her rucksack, turned away. 'Yeah,' she said quietly. 'It's all right for me.'

Georgia saw her to the door. 'Do what you can,' she said. 'And thank you. For caring. For trying.' But it was obvious in her eyes that she never expected to see Benny again.

Benny nodded. 'I'll do what I can,' she assured the woman. 'Good luck.'

The last of the Axis troops were marching from their barracks to the spaceport as Benny approached the Citadel. Stern-faced, immaculately uniformed and marching precisely in step they displayed no regret and no surprise that they were leaving.

There were people on the street, watching as they marched past. Others leaned out of upstairs windows, watching as stoically as the troops themselves. It was not a moment for celebration, not a time to give thanks for the removal of what could so easily have become an army of occupation.

It was a temporary departure. These same stern-faced men with their guns and their lack of feeling would be coming back. Everyone knew that.

They met again in the basement cell.

'We knew that you'd escaped from Straklant,' Gresham told Benny. 'The waiter was a spy. A sad case called Lavers dressed up and listening to the bar gossip for the Axis forces.'

'I gathered,' Benny said. 'What happened to him?'

'You don't want to know,' Luci said quickly. 'The important thing is that the Fifth Axis forces are leaving. Expelled.'

'And Straklant?' Benny asked.

'We've put out a warrant for his arrest,' Gresham said. 'While he didn't actually kill Lavers himself, there are enough witnesses to make a good case for his being an accessory to murder. To say the least. We've expelled the forces and withdrawn what diplomatic immunity they had, so we can arrest him.'

'As soon as we find him,' Luci added. 'So far he's not been on any of the evacuation ships.'

'He won't be,' Benny told them. 'He's going to the Tomb of Rablev.'

Gresham leaned forward, eager. 'You know where it is, then?'

'No,' Benny confessed. 'But he does.' And she told them what she and Georgia had discovered.

'We need to find him,' Luci said when Benny had finished.

'I agree,' Benny said. 'We need to scour the city. Every-available-man job.'

Gresham was looking concerned. 'It isn't that easy,' he said. 'We know the invasion is imminent. You only need to look at the space traffic reports to see the sort of forces they're bringing in. I can't weaken the defence stations and take troops from what will be the front line just to look for Straklant.'

Benny was surprised. 'But even now you know what he's doing? That he's out to disable your entire defences.'

'He's one man,' Gresham pointed out.

'He's pretty handy,' Benny snapped back, grimacing immediately at her choice of phrase. 'If one man can do it, it's probably Straklant.'

'I agree with Benny,' Luci said.

'It makes no difference,' Gresham responded. 'I still won't get authority to free up any of my men.' He stood up. 'What do I really have to go on?' he asked as he paced up and down. 'The suspicions of a known counterfeiter and an off-world archaeologist based on a legendary manuscript.'

'Half a legendary manuscript,' Benny said.

Gresham shook his head. 'Well, there you are then.' He sighed. 'I'll strengthen the guard on the defence installations and control section here in the Citadel. That I can justify.'

'And if it isn't enough?' Benny asked.

'Nothing we can do will be enough,' Gresham said. 'We've always known that. It's pragmatism and compromise the whole way. Whatever we do is always the least worst of our options.' He looked away, his voice quieter now as he said: 'Legend tells us that if the Tomb of Rablev is opened, it will mean the end of the world. If what you say is right, that may indeed turn out to be the case.'

'And you're saying it's down to me to stop it,' Benny told him. 'Just me. Well,' she thought, 'me and Joseph.'

Luci and Gresham exchanged glances. 'Who's Joseph?' they both asked together.

Benny grinned. 'Don't worry,' she assured them, 'he's pretty much useless anyway. She grabbed her rucksack and pulled out the spherical robot. When she tossed him into the air, Joseph bobbed about happily, as if glad to be free.

Gresham and Luci watched expectantly. They were about to be disappointed.

'So, what can you do to help me?' Benny asked. She knew that it was probably an unfair question. But if she could make the point that she really was on her own, then maybe Gresham would find her some real help. It didn't have to be much, after all. Just a few big men with big guns.

'I can reset your wrist chronometer, Professor Summerfield,' Joseph offered. 'I see,' he added huffily, 'that it is eleven seconds behind accurate local time.'

Benny smiled at Gresham as she saw his face fall. 'Thanks,' she said to Joseph, looking still at Gresham. 'That will be a big help.' She smiled. 'He's good at watches,' she told them.

There was a knock at the door before either Luci or Gresham could comment.

Gresham apologised: 'Normally they'd call me, but of

course we're shielded in here.' He went to open the door.

Outside a militia man was standing breathless. He saluted and handed Gresham a folded slip of paper.

Gresham gestured for the man to come in, and shut the door behind him. Then he unfolded the paper and quickly read the message. 'When was this?' he asked.

'Just now, sir. I brought it straight away.'

'And you maintained silent routine?'

'Of course, sir. Even though they've gone, they may have left remote monitoring equipment behind.'

'Good news?' Benny asked brightly.

'I think so, actually,' Gresham said. 'We've intercepted a transmission to the Axis Forces. To Kendrick's command ship in the buffer zone, actually.'

'From Straklant?' Luci asked eagerly.

Gresham nodded. 'Almost certainly. It was sent direct to Kendrick, an ordinary agent wouldn't have that sort of clearance.'

'So, what's it say?' Benny demanded.

'I have no idea. It's in code.'

Benny considered this. 'And that helps us, how exactly?'

Gresham was smiling now. 'We're not as backward as the Fifth Axis think. We don't have all their codes, though we have decrypted their command transmissions. We just don't know what frequencies to monitor for the correct information. We know that they monitor us, even within this building, so we can spread disinformation. And,' he said, 'we can triangulate their own transmissions to determine within a few yards where they're coming from.'

'Usually, we don't need to,' the militia man said. 'Because we know where they are.'

'You're saying you know where this signal is coming from?' Benny said.

'We do,' Gresham confirmed. 'We know where Straklant is.'

'Then let's go and get him,' Luci said.

'We?' Benny asked. 'I thought it was just me and Joseph on this one.'

'I don't work for Gresham, I'm not on the staff,' Luci retorted. 'Where I go and what I do is up to me.' Her voice and her eyes were hard. 'Straklant and I have things to settle,' she said grimly. 'Where is he?'

Kolonel Daglan Straklant was at that moment in the basement of a detached residence just outside the Citadel perimeter. Had Benny looked from the battlements to the West side, she would have been able to see the roof of the building. Maybe she might even have caught a glimpse of the bodies in the upstairs room, where Straklant had taken them at gunpoint, to get them out of his way. He had shot all three of them in the head before making his way down to the basement.

He dragged the accumulated junk and stored possessions from the back wall of the basement, and placed explosives along the length of it. A wave-cancellation suppression field kept the sound of the blast to a minimum. Even so, the whole building rocked noticeably as the charges detonated.

When the smoke cleared, Straklant could see that the wall was gone. Beyond it was mud, earth, sandy soil. He placed the next set of charges, adjusted the field and continued the process.

The whole time, his microwave link to Kendrick was open, and he delivered a running commentary. The signal was faint, but it still got through. He was confident that even if it were to be intercepted by the primitive surveillance and monitoring technology that Kasagrad had, the real-time quadruple key encryption would keep it secure.

The fifth blast revealed a doorway. It was closed off with rough stone, the front chipped and scraped by the explosion. Straklant recognised it from the original version of the photograph to which Jason and Mikey had been added. Such a simple deception, he mused as he pulled away debris. Simply to add Jason would have been too neat. Adding a further person, that had made it all the more credible. Straklant was an expert at deception and he enjoyed the privileged position of knowledge it invariably afforded him.

'I'm in,' he told Kendrick over the link. He had to shout into the lapel mike to make himself heard.

Kendrick's reply was barely audible in his earpiece. 'Excellent. You are confident that you can complete your mission?'

'Of course, sir.'

'Then I shall order the attack to proceed with the assumption that the defence grid will be shut down according to schedule. You know the command frequency?'

Straklant smiled, heaving aside a fallen lump of stone. 'Indeed I do,' he confirmed. Only he and Kendrick knew it at the moment. But as soon as the attack began, it would be keyed to all the assault ships and relayed to their commanders. Straklant would be able to monitor the comms traffic – the actual invasion signals, not the misinformation and rubbish that would simultaneously be broadcast on other frequencies.'

'Don't fail us,' Kendrick said. It sounded more like a warning than a request.

'I shall be at your side when you accept their surrender,' Straklant shouted.

'I look forward to that,' Kendrick replied. For once, Straklant thought as he disconnected the link, his commanding officer had sounded as if he meant it.

By the time that Benny and Luci arrived at the house, Straklant was gone.

There was no answer when they knocked loudly at the door. When they pushed, the door opened, the lock already splintered from its mounting. The two women exchanged looks. The door to the basement was open, steps leading down into the dimly-lit area below.

'Be careful,' Luci mouthed to Benny.

'Thanks,' she murmured back. 'I'd never have thought of that.' She pushed in front of Luci Yendipp and led the way cautiously down the steps.

The whole basement area was foggy with dust. It seemed to hang in the air and catch at the back of Benny's throat as she made her murky way to where the back wall of the building had been.

'Let's hope he isn't hiding waiting for us,' Luci said quietly.

'Let's hope the house doesn't collapse on top of us,' Benny told her. She was speaking at normal volume. 'He got through this wall a while ago, we'd have heard otherwise. He's long gone.'

'Then we need to catch up.' Luci started to walk briskly towards the ragged opening in the ground, but Benny grabbed her arm and pulled her back.

'Me first,' she said. 'I have at least some idea of what we might find down there.' Squaring her shoulders, she stepped into the darkness beyond. 'I've got a flashlight in here somewhere,' she said, rummaging in her rucksack.

'What we'll find,' Luci said as Benny searched, 'is Straklant.'

The flashlight came on. Its beam cut through the swirling dust, illuminating a plain stone corridor that sloped downwards into the tomb.

'We should be able to catch him up,' Benny said confidently.

'What makes you think that?'

For an answer, Benny stooped down and shone the flashlight at the wall near the ground. A sharp spike of corroded metal was sticking out of the stonework. 'He has to avoid the traps,' she said. 'He stood on that slab there, and this shot out to get him.'

'Pity it didn't manage,' Luci said.

'I expect it was old and worn and slow and noisy.' Benny smiled thinly. 'Bit like us.'

'Speak for yourself.' Luci stepped forwards into the gloom.

Again Benny yanked her back, just as the sound of tiny, sharp darts whipped through the air ahead of them. 'I didn't say he'd set off all the traps,' Benny pointed out. 'Just enough to slow down the amateur. A professional, of course, will have no problem,' she said with just a hint of pride.

'Of course,' Luci said, allowing Benny to take the lead. 'I was forgetting that you've read the manuscript.'

'Allow me some illusions, why don't you?' Benny murmured.

But Luci was already adding: 'And you're forgetting, so has he.'

Benny had been expecting the tomb to be a similar stone construction to Ancient Egypt or the underground necropolis of Gakranojen. But although the entrance tunnel lived up to these expectations, it soon became clear that the main structure was of an entirely different construction.

Not only did the floor give way to plates of scratched and tarnished metal, sand and earth blown across them, but the walls too became smooth plates of the same dull material.

Benny paused at the point where the flooring changed. At the edges of the corridor there were signs that a door had once been fixed in position here. A clearer delineation of change. A few feet further in, more heavy hinges bore witness to another set of doors that had been removed.

'Who do you suppose took them out?' Luci asked when Benny showed her.

'Not Goram and Lacey,' Benny replied. 'There's nothing in what I've seen of their notes and records. And they knew what they were doing – nicking the main doors wasn't their sort of thing at all. No,' she decided, 'this happened much earlier I think.'

Further down the passageway, Benny shone her flashlight along the walls. Symbols and crude drawings were etched into the metal, the deep cuts standing out like dried blood where they had become rusty.

'These are later too,' Benny said. 'That's why they've tarnished. The metal was treated before they were cut in.'

'Which tells us what?' Luci asked. 'Not that I'm really interested.' They were still hurrying along – torn between the need for haste and the caution engendered by the knowledge that death might be waiting round any corner. Death in the form of a trap to dissuade grave robbers, or Kolonel Straklant.

'It confirms that the structure was here before it was used as a tomb. Which links in with the legend.' Benny paused to examine a section of wall. 'Look, here.'

The pictograms showed figures being dragged down a hole in the ground, a sloping tunnel into a shallow hillside. Further along was a cut-away view of the inside of the tomb, doors being slammed shut on stick-figures that struggled to escape. Above and behind the main picture stood a crude representation of the Citadel. Behind that were fields full of wilting and dying crops, bodies strewn across the minimalist landscape.

'Rablev was entombed with the symbol of his power, remember,' Benny said. 'She pointed to the area beyond the Citadel. 'The gods grew angry with his presumption, and the ground became poisoned. Thousands, maybe even millions died.'

'In the legend,' Luci said. 'Right?'

'In the picture here,' Benny said. 'Which gives us contemporary evidence that something happened.' She moved her finger along to a room at the far end of the drawing, at the deepest level of the tomb. A single figure stood inside the room, its face turned towards them, more finished than other parts of the drawing. The face was torn apart with a scream of terror. 'Want to bet that's Rablev?'

'You really think there's something in it?' Luci asked as they hurried on. 'You really think there's a chance that if we open the inner chamber the world will end because of some ancient superstition?'

'I don't know,' Benny said. 'And I really don't care. So long as we stop Straklant before he opens it, I'm happy just leaving well alone. I thought it was legend at first. But now I think there might be something in it.'

There were doorways set into the walls of the passageway, each blocked either by metal plates or closed off with heavy stonework. So far they had ignored them, concentrating on following the main passageway through towards the innermost chamber. But now they reached a doorway where the stonework had crumbled away. There was a hole, several feet across, in the middle section of the door.

Benny took the flashlight and approached the hole.

'Do we have time for this?' Luci asked. Her voice was a whisper, full of nerves.

Benny whispered back. 'Maybe not. But I want to be sure that Straklant isn't hiding in there. I don't like the idea of him sneaking up behind us.'

'Right.' Luci beckoned for Benny to shine the flashlight through the hole in the doorway. She raised her gun, standing ready beside the doorway, poised to take aim at anything that moved. 'Now!' she said.

Benny swung the flashlight up and into the room beyond the door. At the same moment Luci stepped across, tracking the beam of light with the gun.

They both screamed.

A face stared back at them through the hole. A face bleached white, black empty sockets for eyes, teeth drawn into a grin where lips and flesh should have been. A single claw-like hand reached out towards them, frozen in the torchlight, fingers long and thin, joints cracked. As they watched, the skull shifted slightly, perhaps disturbed by their movement. It seemed to collapse in on itself, the teeth buckling and the empty eyes slowly cracking open as the face shattered.

Benny and Luci exchanged embarrassed looks.

'I hope he didn't hear us,' Luci said.

Benny sighed. 'I've been poking about in bone pits for longer than I like to remember, but the old dust-to-dust skeleton routine gets me every time.'

'By my reckoning,' Benny whispered, 'the chamber he's heading for is about thirty yards further along. She clicked off the flashlight. But they could see no sign of a light down the passageway.

'You think he knows we're coming?'

'Of course he does,' the voice said.

The light dazzled them, shining directly into their eyes from very close. Behind it, as her eyes began to cope, Benny could make out Straklant's silhouette.

'I should think everyone down here knows you're coming. You've been making enough noise to wake the dead.' He seemed to find this amusing, a wry chuckle coming from behind the light.

The light moved as he motioned them forwards. 'You're just in time to help.'

'Oh yes?' Benny said.

'Oh yes. You see, I have a slight quandary here.'

Benny's eyes were able to cope now and she could make out some of the features of Straklant's face as he smiled at them. It wasn't a pleasant sight, she decided.

'This door,' he gestured with the flashlight, 'leads to the chamber that I am interested in.'

'Oh,' Benny said with forced levity, 'you mean where the vents are which you hope will get you into the Citadel to sabotage the defence grid? That chamber?'

She was pleased to see that Straklant frowned. 'You're better than I thought,' he said quietly. 'But you're still too late to stop me.'

'I wouldn't prejudge that,' Luci said.

Benny glanced at her, and saw that the gun had disappeared. She wondered where the woman had hidden it, raised an eyebrow in question. But she got no response.

'I can manage without you,' Straklant said. 'So I suggest you shut up. And you, Benny,' he said, turning back to her.

'My friends call me Benny,' she told him. 'I'm Professor Summerfield to you.'

He seemed not at all distracted. 'And you, Professor Summerfield,' he went on immediately, 'will open this door for me. Otherwise I kill her.' He motioned with the gun at Luci. 'And then,' he said, 'I kill you.'

'How will that help? And how were you proposing to open the door without me anyway?'

For an answer, Strakland pulled a cylinder from his jacket pocket. It was stubby, gleaming metal, fitting easily in his hand. 'Demolition charge,' he said. 'But it does run the risk – the slight risk – of being heard in the Citadel above us. I'd rather not give them any warning of my visit.' He returned the charge to his pocket. 'Open the door,' he ordered.

'Sure you want to do this?' Benny asked. 'After all, open the tomb and it's the end of the world.'

'Don't open it,' he said, 'and it's the end of you.'

Benny sighed. 'Fair enough. I'll give it a go.' She turned and started walking down the passageway, away from the door.

'Stop!' he ordered. 'Come back here. Now.'

Benny stopped, and sighed loudly. She was on the other side of Straklant from Luci now, maybe she would be able to get her gun without him seeing. But even as Benny congratulated herself on this move, Straklant grabbed the woman and pushed her down the passage after Benny.

'Where are you going?' he demanded.

'You know,' she said, trying to sound annoyed as well as apprehensive, 'you really don't know a thing about archaeology, do you?'

He levelled the gun. 'I hope you aren't wasting my time,' he warned.

'Look, the doors to the main chamber are just down here,' Benny told him. 'They will be bigger and grander than this one, and they have already been opened at least once – by Goram and Lacey.'

'So? I'm not interested in the main chamber.'

'Well, you should be,' Benny shot back. 'Because quite apart from the threat of death and destruction If we open them, it will be easier to determine what the mechanism is, and maybe what tricks and traps lie behind the doors. There should be evidence of how Goram and Lacey got in, and perhaps some clues as to what they actually found. Unless,' she added 'you already know from the manuscript how to open the doors, which I doubt as you just asked me to do it.'

The gun wavered slightly and she could tell he was going for it. Benny had no plan as such, she just wanted to delay him, get a chance to think, maybe a chance for Luci to use the gun.

'Once I've seen the doors to the main chamber then – maybe – I'll be able to open that one for you.' She turned slowly and continued down the passage. 'But no promises,' she called back.

'I have a promise for you,' Straklant called after her, his footsteps loud on the metal flooring as he followed. 'Try to trick me and I'll kill you. Try to stop me and I'll kill you. Try to waste my time and I'll kill you.'

Benny was at the doors now. She set her flashlight down on the ground, so that it cast her shadow large and grotesque across the heavy door. 'Look,' she said as she ran her hands over the metal, 'do you want my help or not?'

'Just get on with it,' he said. Straklant pushed Luci over towards Benny. Luci resisted a moment, catching hold of Straklant's jacket and digging her feet in. But he dropped his flashlight and prised her fingers away with his free hand, lifted her, and flung her across to Benny.

For a moment, as Luci staggered, as she fell beside Benny, as Benny turned from the doors to see what was happening, Luci flashed a glimpse of the demolition charge. Then she closed her hand round it, sitting on the floor, with the hand behind her back. Benny could see the shadowy form of her hand as it pushed the charge up against the door.

'I think we'd do better to open the tomb, destroy the world, than let it be invaded by the likes of him,' she said.

Straklant ignored her. 'For what it's worth,' he said as he retrieved his flashlight and swung it to illuminate the heavy doors, 'I have never wanted your help. Don't mistake necessity for choice.'

Benny was barely listening. The metal of these doors was not as cold as the others. She ran her hands over the uneven surface, pressing, feeling. It was a softer, heavier construction. Somewhere inside her memory something stirred, some semblance of recognition. She pulled off her rucksack and tossed it to one side.

Straklant was still talking, over her thoughts. 'I didn't want to come to Braxiatel. I didn't enjoy making your acquaintance and chasing round after the manuscript.'

'Ah, you're just saying that,' Benny told him. It was an automatic response. Her mind was racing now. Metal floors and walls. A central passageway with rooms off it, and a chamber at the end that had heavier doors. The double doors that had been at the entrance. The position of the entrance, towards the top of the main passageway but not at its end...

And as most of her mind was occupied with the problem, another part of it suddenly clicked other elements into place.

'You came to Braxiatel to find me,' she heard herself say out loud. 'You needed Braxiatel and me to find the other half of the manuscript, whether you liked it or not.'

'True,' he admitted.

'Which means you already knew what was in the first half, Goram's half. You knew about the vents.'

'But we didn't know the location of the tomb,' he said. 'You're very clever suddenly. When it's too late.'

'Just working things out,' she said. She turned, catching Luci's inquiring eye for a moment through the gloom. 'I know where we are,' she murmured. Then she returned her attention to the doors, talking to distract him as she rubbed at the left hand door about two thirds of the way up. 'You had already doctored the Goram half of the manuscript, hadn't you? All except the picture of Jason – you had to add that to ensure I'd come along. Clever of you to dirty it down and stick him in the shadows so I didn't recognise it. I don't know how you knew that Jason was important to me, but you did.' The symbol – it must be on here. That was where Goram and Lacey had seen it. 'So you got the picture, and you tricked me.'

There it was. Through the grim and dust of the years she could see the circular symbol emerging as her hand became progressively more dirty. She laughed out loud, covering at once: 'You tricked Braxiatel too, not many people manage that. He thought it was his own fault there was no catalogue entry for the manuscript, but of course there wasn't. Because…'

'Because the manuscript was never in his collection.'

'Nobody was stealing anything that night,' Benny said. 'It wasn't poor Dale Pettit who broke in and got caught. It was you. He was the one who was lost, you were the one breaking in. Putting the manuscript into the Collection where you could then arrange for one of us to find it. Am I right?'

'Something like that.' He actually sounded impressed. 'Pettit was a stroke of luck. He speeded things up for me.'

'He died for you,' Benny snapped back. 'You killed him and we thanked you for it,' she said bitterly. 'In fact the only thing I do have to thank you for was finding Wolsey when he was hurt. Another piece of luck, it meant you could get to me and take the picture of Jason.'

'Who's Wolsey?' Luci asked.

Benny realised Luci had said it to attract her attention, to tell or show her something. Luci's hand was edging closer to the demolition charge against the door. But then a new realisation overtook Benny. 'We have to get out of here,' she said. 'We have to get away from here and seal it up. Or it really will be the end of the world.'

'He's her unpleasant little cat,' Straklant said, ignoring her.

'Aren't you listening,' Benny shouted. 'Don't you realise where we are? What Rablev's power was?'

Straklant laughed. 'A pathetic little creature. It whined and bleated as much as she does.'

'This is a spaceship!' Benny shouted back, angrily. 'We're in the main transom. The construction, the design, everything tells us that. And in here,' she turned and thumped the doors, 'in here is the power that Rablev harnessed.'

'Can you stand pain?' Straklant shouted above her. 'Because he couldn't, you know.' He raised the gun. 'I've wasted enough time indulging you.'

'Look!' Benny was thumping her fist against the symbol she had uncovered on the door. A circle, cut into six sectors shaded alternately a faded yellow and a grimy black. 'Take it from me, if we aren't careful we'll unleash the destructive force that Rablev did. He found the crashed ship, and he thought he could control it, tame it with a little knowledge. And maybe he did for a while.'

'What do you mean?' Luci demanded.

Straklant primed the gun. A heavy, dull click that echoed off the walls.

'Then something went wrong. The ship's reactor went critical. Meltdown, maybe. The radiation leaked out and poisoned the air and the ground. People died from the sickness. So they sealed it up again and slowly, very slowly, things recovered.'

'You're bluffing,' Straklant said calmly as he took aim.

Luci's hand clenched on the canister behind her.

'No, I'm not,' Benny said. 'Damage those doors and the radiation will escape again. Goram and Lacey sealed the tomb behind them when they came in. That bit you left intact – there was a sandstorm, remember. They didn't know it but they created an airlock. Limited contamination. But there was enough to kill them both. Just be thankful they sealed this chamber behind them when they left.'

'I still say you're bluffing.' He was grinning behind the flashlight. 'You can't take it. Any more than your cat could.'

'Wolsey?' Benny frowned. Then her mind cleared and she realised what he had been saying. And somehow that was worse than knowing what was behind the doors. 'You hurt Wolsey,' she breathed.

He laughed. The flashlight moved slightly as he watched her.

'It wasn't chance at all. You found Wolsey, and you deliberately hurt him. You broke his paw just so that you could get to see me.'

'Benny,' Luci warned in a low voice.

But Benny ignored her. She was shouting, screaming, didn't know what she was saying or doing. Somehow she was in mid air, launching herself towards the beam of light and the grotesque smile behind it.

It surprised him. The flashlight went rolling away. The gun clattered to the metal floor. A mêlée of arms and legs, pounding, thrashing, punching, kicking.

Then a flashlight, Benny's flashlight, was pointed right at them.

'Stop it. Now!'

The beam moved as Straklant disentangled himself from Benny and stepped away. 'I wouldn't do that,' he said calmly. But there was an uneasy edge to his voice.

Luci was holding the canister. She stood in front of the doors, the charge raised for them to see, the flashlight in her other hand. 'Better to destroy the world than allow your kind to take it,' she said.

'No, Luci – please,' Benny said. 'You have no idea. Have you seen what radiation poisoning can do? How long it takes to die, how it happens?'

'I've seen what his people do,' Luci said. 'I've seen how people die when the Fifth Axis arrive.' She wiped her eyes with the back of her hand, the flashlight beam jiggering across the passageway as she moved. 'And that won't happen here.'

As the flashlight moved, so did Straklant. He was falling, rolling, coming up with his gun and aiming straight at Benny, hands up high so that it pointed at her head.

And he was smiling. 'You can throw away the charge,' he said over his shoulder to Luci. Without the key sequence you can't prime it. It's useless to you.' Then he turned back to Benny. 'For what it's worth,' he said, 'I enjoyed hurting your cat.'

'For what it's worth,' Benny replied quietly, 'I told you never to raise your hands to a lady.' Her knee was already moving as she spoke, driving upwards with all her force. 'The reason being,' she said calmly, reasonably, as he slumped to one side with a shrill cry of intense pain, 'that it leaves your groin unprotected.'

He rolled on the floor, his face contorted in the dull glow from Luci's flashlight. But he still had the gun, and he was slowly bringing it round to face Benny. Through the agony and the tears of pain he was still smiling.

At the end of the passageway, Luci was throwing the canister. It spun lazily in the air, skimming across the lead surface of the shielded doors. As it spun away, she pulled her own gun from the small of her back.

Benny sighed with relief. 'Shoot him, Luci!' she heard herself screaming. 'Quickly, end it. End it now!'

But Luci wasn't aiming at Straklant. Benny's face froze and the words died in her throat as she saw the woman swing round, bring the gun up, aim it at the spinning canister as the charge bounced against the radiation warning symbol on the doorway.

A flash from the gun.

A ghostly-white flare of released energy.

The doors crashing open to reveal the dead darkness beyond.

Benny sinking to her knees.

Straklant shouting something that was lost in the noise of the blast.

Luci spinning away, caught full in the explosion.

Benny's vision blurring as the world came to an end.

12
Treachery

The world began with a light.

Kolonel Daglan Straklant recovered consciousness to discover he was lying on his back. He was used to the feeling of disorientation, he knew it would pass. The light was burning into his eyes and he blinked as he tried to focus. He rolled, staggered to his feet, and saw that the light came from a flashlight that was lying on the ground.

When he lost his hand to the enemy barrage on Celestos, he had lost his consciousness with it. He could still remember the disbelief and detachment he had felt when he came round, staring down at the stump of his wrist. The memory would return in a few moments. It always did.

He looked round, staring into the gloom of the passageway for several seconds before he stooped to recover the flashlight. A pair of heavy doors lay angled against the walls beside him, blown out by the explosion. A body – a young woman's body – lay crumpled and broken beside one of them. She was obviously dead, but he checked for a pulse anyway. She was holding a gun and he prised it from her fingers, checking the charge and keeping it aimed with the beam of light.

Memory returned in a rush as he turned to face back down the corridor. And with it, realisation:

The world had not ended when the doors were opened.

Benny was nowhere to be seen.

He had a job to do. The success of the invasion was assured, but his mission was to make that success as swift and simple as possible.

He started back down the passageway. After the noise from the explosion of the demolition charge, he no longer needed to worry about opening the door to the chamber silently. He had several more charges. It was time to get to work.

Time.

How long had he been unconscious? How long did he have?

He checked his wrist chronometer. And his heart skipped a beat. He had been unconscious for over five hours.

Five hours.

The invasion was already underway. Well advanced if all was going well. The defence grid was unlikely still to be an issue, and the Citadel control room would be heavily guarded and manned by now.

Even as he played through his choices, even as he decided that his best option was to get out of the tomb and meet up with the invading Axis forces, Straklant heard the sound of people approaching. Marching. In step.

He ducked into the shadows and turned off his flashlight.

There were three figures approaching. Two of them were orderly, marching, holding flashlights. The third – a woman – was stumbling in front of them, pushed forwards.

'Where is he?' the tallest of them demanded, addressing the woman.

'He's down here, somewhere. I told you.'

Straklant recognised her voice – Benny. At the same moment, he recognised the uniforms of the two men herding her along the passageway. Fifth Axis officers – a Field Commander and a Lieutenant by the look of it. He stepped out of the shadows in time to catch hold of Benny as she stumbled and almost fell.

'Is that him?' the Commander demanded, talking to Benny rather than Straklant.

She nodded, pulling away from Straklant and folding her arms. 'Yes,' she said. 'Can I go now?'

The Commander gave a short laugh and turned to Straklant. 'You are Kolonel Daglan Straklant?' he barked.

'Of course,' Straklant said. 'I'm glad you're here.'

'Are you?'

He didn't sound glad himself. And why didn't he address Straklant as 'sir'?

But before Straklant could comment, the Commander went on. 'I'm not. The entrance to this place has collapsed, so we're blocked in. Three of my men are somewhere under the rubble.' He looked at Benny accusingly.

'I told you,' she snapped, 'it wasn't my fault. You can't blow up the foundations of a building and not expect it to collapse eventually. I'm as sorry as you are that we're stuck down here. Except that I was dead already.' She turned to Straklant. 'Just as he is.'

'What do you mean?' he asked. But already, he knew.

'The radiation,' she said. 'We've been soaking up rads for nearly six hours. I give us a couple of days at best.'

'We have to get out of here,' Straklant said. His mind was still struggling to cope with this information.

'My men are digging,' the Commander said. 'But it will take time. Maybe too long for us. Certainly too long for you.' He sighed loudly. 'I just wanted to see your face before we're all dead. I wanted to look a traitor in the eye, and know that he is dying.'

'Traitor?' Straklant took a step backwards. 'What do you mean?'

The Lieutenant was shining his flashlight into Straklant's eyes, dazzling him as the Commander spoke. 'If you weren't already as good as dead, I'd kill you myself.' His voice was angry and bitter. 'Have you any idea how many good people have died because of what you've done?'

'What?' he shouted back. 'What have I done?'

'As if he doesn't know,' the Lieutenant said quietly. He also sounded bitter, resigned.

'Yeah, come on Daglan,' Benny said. 'The game's up. They know all about you being one of our agents here on Kasagrad.'

'What?'

'They know you were working for us all the time. Setting this up.'

Straklant shook his head. 'No,' he said forcefully. 'No, that's not true! Whatever she's told you, it's lies. She's making it all up – can't you see that? Don't listen to her!'

'I don't,' the Commander said. 'I don't need to.' His voice was low, dangerous.

'Take me to Kendrick,' Straklant said. 'Get us out of here and take me to Kendrick. He'll tell you.'

'Maybe he doesn't know?' the Lietenant suggested, shifting the flashlight slightly so that now Straklant could at least make out their silhouettes behind the glare.

'Oh he knows. Kendrick's dead,' the Commander said. 'You knew that. You set him up.'

'Look,' Straklant tried to remain calm. 'There's some misunderstanding here. I don't know what you think, or what this bitch has told you.'

'Charming,' Benny murmured. 'Hardly the way to talk to your controller.'

He tried to ignore her. 'What's your name?' he asked the Commander. 'Why are you here?'

'I am Commander Graves. And my mission is to apprehend the traitor Daglan Straklant, formerly a Kolonel in the Fifth Axis Security Elite. Dead or alive. I was given your last triangulated position according to your voice transmissions, and here we are.'

Straklant's eyes had adjusted to the glare and he could see that Graves was smiling thinly.

'But I am not a traitor,' he said.

'The evidence suggests otherwise.'

'What evidence?'

Graves sighed, as if he knew he was telling Straklant what he already knew but was willing for the moment to play along. 'Your mission was supposedly to knock out the Kasagrad defence grid. That has not happened.'

'So I failed in my mission. But the invasion still went ahead. That's not something I shall be proud of, but it's hardly treason.'

Graves went on: 'The attack frequency codes were released only to yourself and Marshal Kendrick.'

'That's standard practice,' Straklant said angrily.

'It is also standard practice for the secondary officer to confirm those codes to the battlefield comms system ahead of the attack in case the primary officer is unable to do so.' Graves took a step forward, clearly visible in the light now as he faced Straklant. 'You did not do so.'

'I was unconscious,' Straklant shot back. 'Does it matter?'

Graves watched him closely for a moment. He seemed to be trying to control his anger. He was a tall man, taller than Straklant, his features finely chiselled and formed into an expression that was part sneer, part anger. 'Does it matter?' he demanded. 'This operation is going to hell, and you ask me if it matters?' He shook his head. 'I should execute you here and now. But I'd rather get you back to the fleet, if you're still alive. If we can get out of here in time to rejoin the retreat.'

'Retreat?' Straklant felt cold suddenly. For the first time he began to feel out of control, that there was more to this than he knew.

The Lieutenant's voice was calmer, but there was still a strained quality to it. 'Marshal Kendrick's command ship was destroyed in a pre-emptive attack minutes ahead of the invasion.'

'Before he released the command codes,' Graves said. 'But when the forces were already committed. And so the attack went ahead, in the knowledge that the codes would be confirmed by the secondary officer on the ground.' His hand lashed out and his index finger stopped just short of Straklant's eye. 'You!'

'But – but, I didn't know,' Straklant said. He could feel the blood draining from his face.

'Somebody identified Kendrick's ship to the enemy,' Graves said. He took a step towards Straklant, who stepped back. 'Somebody failed to release the attack frequency codes for the operation when we were committed to the battle.' Another step. 'Somebody failed to disable the defence grid so that our fleet, already flying blind without instructions or a credible command structure, flew straight into it.

Somebody,' he said, 'is found skulking around in an underground tomb with his enemy contact hoping to loot a few more relics for his private collection.'

'No, no that's not it.' Another step backwards. And Straklant found himself pressed against the wall of the passage.

'And meanwhile our fleet is still flying blind, still unable to co-ordinate its attack, unable even to retreat or regroup. Because,' Graves said, his face close to Straklant's, his hand pressed to the wall beside Straklant's head, 'you haven't released the codes the computers are expecting to use.'

Graves stepped back suddenly and grabbed Straklant's right arm, yanking it upwards. He pulled the uniform sleeve back to reveal his skin beneath. Straklant gasped. It was red and raw, scarred and pitted. And suddenly his arm felt as numb as his brain.

Across the passageway, Benny held up her own arm, showed him the same scarring across it. As she turned, Straklant could see that her face was also blistered down one side. 'Sorry it had to end like this, my friend,' she said calmly. 'But at least we defeated them. The two of us.'

'You –' Straklant pushed away from the wall, reaching out for her, incoherent in his rage.

But Graves slammed him back into the wall with sudden and unexpected force. 'At least you will die a traitor,' he hissed. 'Everyone knows what you did. You'll go down in history dishonoured, as the man who betrayed the Fifth Axis.'

'No!' Straklant screamed. 'The codes – I can give you the codes! There's still time, there has to be.'

Graves turned away. 'I should just let you die down here,' he said. 'What good are the codes now? Even if we could trust you to give us the right ones.' He started to walk away, back towards the blocked entrance. 'Bring the woman,' he said to the Lieutenant as he passed.

'Sir. And the traitor?'

'I am not a traitor!' Straklant shouted. 'I am an officer of the Fifth Axis Security Elite.'

The Lieutenant took Benny's arm and led her away. Graves turned back to Straklant.

'No, you're not,' he said quietly. 'Not any more.' He reached out and pulled Straklant's comms-pin from his lapel. Then he dropped it to the floor and ground his heel down on it, without looking.

For several seconds Straklant stood shaking with rage and anger. 'I'll tell you the frequency!' he screamed after Graves. But the officer did not even hesitate. 'I'm not a traitor! There is still time, there has to be.' He ran after Graves, grabbed his shoulder and turned him round. 'Fifty-three centibels,' he said, breathless. 'The frequency is fifty-three –'

But Graves was not looking at Straklant. His eyes had dropped to the hand clamped on his shoulder. Graves reached up and pulled it away, as if it was something unpleasant that had dropped there. Only then did he glance up at Straklant. For a moment their eyes met, for a moment, Straklant thought he could see sadness as well as anger deep within.

Then Commander Graves turned and marched after Benny and the Lieutenant. Leaving Straklant alone in the dark.

He had no idea of time. Maybe it was only a few moments that he stood there, broken and alone. Then he retraced his steps down the passageway, feeling for where he thought he had dropped the flashlight.

He found it at last, switched it on, made his way slowly after Graves and Benny.

The entrance was clear. It looked exactly as he had left it. He sat down on the floor of the basement, dropping the flashlight. How long did he have, he wondered. How long did anyone have now that the radiation was leaking out into the world. He pulled up his sleeve and stared at the raw skin that was exposed.

Somehow, in the light, it seemed less raw. Less scarred. Less like the skin had been eaten away, and more as if something had been stuck over it. He could feel the pit of his stomach dropping away as he slowly reached out and tugged at the edge of the scarred patch; as it slowly pulled free and strung away from the forearm that lay unblemished beneath.

Somewhere at the edge of his vision, in the doorway, a small sphere bobbed in the air. Bizarrely, it cleared its throat. 'Er,' it said in an embarrassed nasal whine, 'I'm afraid your chronometer is five hours and thirty-seven minutes ahead of actual local time. Would you like me to reset it for you?'

'Fifty-three centibels,' the man who was not Commander Graves told Herv Gresham.

'Thank you,' Gresham said. 'Thank you both. With that we have a chance – a good chance – of turning this around.' They were standing in the sunshine on the street outside the house. Gresham excused himself to relay the information. The man who was not a Lieutenant in the Fifth Axis forces but in fact an officer of the Kasagrad Militia went with him.

'You know,' Benny said, 'that's about the first time I think I've seen him smile.'

'Well,' the officer who was not Graves, 'he has a lot to smile about.'

'I was afraid Straklant would recognise your voice.'

'It's amazing what you can achieve with some holo-effects and a uniform.' He took off his officer's cap, and, as he did so, his face wobbled, then changed. It flickered from the face of Commander Graves to the chiselled features that Benny knew so well. 'There's a miniature projector built into the brim,' Braxiatel explained, with a wry smile. 'A bit of disorientation, emotion and good old-fashioned anger helps as well, of course.'

'Were you very angry?' Benny teased.

But he took her seriously. 'When I heard that Josiah Vanderbilt had been killed, yes I was. I was already on my way to warn you when I got Gresham's message.' Braxiatel looked at his Fifth Axis officer's cap for a moment, then tucked it under his arm. 'I feel a little conspicuous in this uniform. I think I'll find somewhere to change, if you don't mind.'

Benny watched Braxiatel follow Gresham to a ground car. She waited a few moments longer, and sure enough Joseph came out of the house, weaving and bobbing his way rapidly towards her.

'Well, really!' the small white sphere exclaimed as it approached.

'I told you he wouldn't appreciate the help,' Benny said. Her rucksack, battered and stained but still largely intact was on the pavement at her feet. She pulled it open, and nodded at it.

'Must I?' Joseph protested.

'You must,' she said. 'By the way, what was the radiation count down there?'

'Minimal,' Joseph responded in a muffled voice as he settled himself into the rucksack. 'A residual background level consistent with a main reactor overload. But it hasn't been at a dangerous level for at least two hundred years.'

Benny hoisted the rucksack on to her shoulder. 'Bad luck for poor old Goram and Lacey,' she murmured. 'A few hundred years later and they could have had the glory they expected. Even if there wasn't actually any treasure.'

She climbed into the car. It drove away.

It was clear almost immediately that something was very wrong. Not only was the defence grid still active, a possibility which Marshal Kendrick had anticipated, but the Kasagrad forces seemed to know his every move. Which he had not.

It was a long time before anyone was willing to believe that the enemy might be using their own comms traffic – actually knowing which frequency to monitor and being able to decode it.

But by the time the retreat was in full swing, by the time Kendrick was forced to admit defeat and signal the Imperator personally to apologise, it was evident to everyone.

Just as it was evident what must have happened and who was to blame.

They picked him up in a small cargo-freighter, trying to run the blockade. It was a blockade in name only by then. With the loss of the Sixth Fleet, all but destroyed in the Kasagrad incident, the Fifth Axis was pulling back from that area of the Territories, evacuating several of the assimilated planets and retreating to the old Merinfast Line.

'So,' Kendrick said when they brought him in, 'the traitor Daglan Straklant, formerly a Kolonel in the Fifth Axis Security Elite.'

He did not reply. He just stood there, his head hung in shame. A broken man.

'Why?' Kendrick asked quietly. 'Why did you betray us? What made you decide to give them the frequency?' He stood up and came round his desk, stopping in front of his former adjutant so that they were face to face. 'I would think you would have stayed there, safe, if it were through choice. But I know they could never have forced it from you. I may never understand it, but I have to conclude...' His voice tailed off.

For a moment they stood facing each other. Then suddenly Kendrick's hand flew up, striking Straklant viciously across the face.

But he showed no pain. Did not react at all. Quietly, in a husky, broken voice he asked: 'How did you find me?'

'There is a locator-transmitter embedded in your hand,' Kendrick told him. He turned and nodded to the two guards standing by the door. 'We've always known exactly where you are.'

He sat down again as the guards dragged Straklant away. 'Just as we both know exactly where you are going now,' he murmured as the door closed behind them. His voice was a hoarse rush of anger as he spat: 'You traitor.'

Braxiatel was leaning back in his chair, looking at his study ceiling. 'You know, it's an odd thing,' he said.

'What is?' Benny took a sip of champagne and watched him swing slowly in his chair.

'That the forgery may end up being worth more than the original Doomsday Manuscript. Given the circumstances.'

Benny nodded. 'Turning point in the war, they're saying.'

Braxiatel wasn't convinced. 'Bit early to tell, I think. But it's changed the balance in terms of morale if nothing else.'

Benny thought of Piccolini, behind his bar, of Mikey slumped at a corner table, of Georgia and her children... and smiled. 'Oh, we've done more than,' she said.

Braxiatel sat upright and looked at her across his desk. 'Yes,' he agreed. 'Yes, we did very well. You did very well. I was merely an actor in your play.'

She laughed. 'If you like.' Another sip of champagne. 'It's good to be back,' she said. 'Having fun.'

'Well, that's what it's all about really,' he told her.

'Yes,' Benny said. 'I suppose it is. Let's just hope we don't have too much fun. There's only so much excitement a girl can stand.'

'Mmm. More champagne?'

'Yeah,' she said. 'Why not?'

Acknowledgments

Writing the first full novel of a new or revamped series means that you have to set up lots of things that you tend not to get enough credit for later. But that's fine – in fact, that's fair. But it wouldn't be fair if I didn't point out that it also means I get to play with ideas and characters that other people don't get enough credit for. Principally that's Gary Russell and Jacqueline Rayner. An editor's job is to make the author look as good as possible. I appreciate the fact that this novel is the richer for their involvement. (And can I have the money now, please?)

Justin Richards, September 2000

About the Author

JUSTIN RICHARDS is an author and editor. He also works as a business and IT consultant, telling people who should know better that they should know better. Justin has written for most media – technical manuals, novels, articles, non-fiction books, audio, and television. But that doesn't seem to stop him.

Also Available

PROFESSOR BERNICE SUMMERFIELD AND THE DEAD MEN DIARIES

A short story collection edited by PAUL CORNELL

ISBN 1-903654-00-9

Who but Professor Bernice Summerfield, interstellar archaeologist, raconteur, boozer and wit, would get other people to write her autobiography – albeit under threat of death from two bounty hunters sent by a publisher far too concerned about little things like deadlines?

These stories are an ideal introduction to the life of Bernice Summerfield: falling off cliffs, getting sacrificed to orange pygmies, saving the universe and trying to buy a new frock.

Cliffhanging escapes! Adventure on distant planets!
Scones for tea!

The anthology includes new stories by SF author Kate Orman, *Queer as Folk* script-editor Matt Jones and Steven Moffat, the creator of *Coupling*, alongside Mark Michalowski, Daniel O'Mahony, Eddie Robson, Cavan Scott & Mark Wright, Dave Stone, Kathryn Sullivan and Caroline Symcox.

Coming Soon

PROFESSOR BERNICE SUMMERFIELD AND THE GODS OF THE UNDERWORLD
A novel by
STEPHEN COLE

ISBN 1-903654-23-8

There's a whisper going round that the long-lost temple of the Argian Gods of the Underworld has finally been discovered on the planet Venedel. There's an even quieter whisper that deep inside it lies the Argian Oracle, an ancient artefact that can pinpoint the whereabouts of any soul in the universe. Benny Summerfield sets out to see if this is true – perhaps it can tell her the whereabouts of her missing ex-husband, Jason Kane.

Venedel, however, is under siege from an over-zealous Federation, starving the planet until the people capitulate to its terms. Despite this, a team of Nishtubi mercenaries are running the blockade to supply aid for the Venedelans. But why? They have nothing to gain.

Caught between jingoistic natives, Nishtubi heavies, a plague of ancient killers and the secrets of the Gods of the Underworld, Benny faces a great deal of trouble – and has nowhere to run…

PRESENTING

PROFESSOR BERNICE SUMMERFIELD

AND THE AUDIO DRAMA SERIES
starring Lisa Bowerman as Benny

Big Finish Productions is proud to present the original Bernice Summerfield adventures on audio, based on novels published originally by Virgin Publishing!

Featuring original music and sound-effects, these full-cast plays are available on CD from all good specialist stores, or via mail order.

1.1 *Oh No It Isn't!*
adapted by Jacqueline Rayner from the novel by Paul Cornell
1.2 *Beyond the Sun*
adapted by Matt Jones from his own novel
1.3 *Walking to Babylon*
adapted by Jacqueline Rayner from the novel by Kate Orman
1.4 *Birthright*
adapted by Jacqueline Rayner from the novel by Nigel Robinson
1.5 *Just War*
adapted by Jacqueline Rayner from the novel by Lance Parkin
1.6 *Dragons' Wrath*
adapted by Jacqueline Rayner from the novel by Justin Richards

And coming soon, brand-new fully original audio dramas

2.1 *Professor Bernice Summerfield and the Secret of Cassandra*
by David Bailey
2.2 *Professor Bernice Summerfield and the Extinction Event*
by Lance Parkin
2.3 *Professor Bernice Summerfield and the Stone's Lament*
by Mike Tucker
2.4 *Professor Bernice Summerfield and the Skymines of Karthos*
by David Bailey

If you wish to order the CD version, please contact
PO Box 1127, Maidenhead, Berkshire. SL6 3LN.
Big Finish Hotline 01628 828283.
Delivery within 28 days of release.

For more details visit our website at
http://www.bernicesummerfield.com

PRESENTING

DOCTOR WHO

AN ALL-NEW AUDIO DRAMA

Big Finish Productions is proud to present all-new *Doctor Who* adventures on audio!

Featuring original music and sound-effects, these full-cast plays are available on double cassette in high street stores, and on limited-edition double CD from all good specialist stores, or via mail order.

Available from November 2000

THE HOLY TERROR

A four-part story by Robert Shearman.
Starring **Colin Baker** as the Doctor
and **Robert Jezek** as Frobisher.

The TARDIS lands in a forbidding castle in a time of religious upheaval. The old god has been overthrown, and all heretics are to be slaughtered. Obviously it isn't the sort of thing which would happen there every day – just every few years or so.

Soon after the Doctor and Frobisher are hailed as messengers from heaven, they become vital to opposing factions in their struggle for power. But will they be merely the acolytes of the new order – or will they be made gods themselves?

If you wish to order the CD version, please contact
PO Box 1127, Maidenhead, Berkshire. SL6 3LN.
Big Finish Hotline 01628 828283.
Delivery within 28 days of release.

Other stories featuring the Sixth Doctor still available include:
The Sirens of Time   *Whispers of Terror*
The Marian Conspiracy   *The Apocalypse Element*
The Spectre of Lanyon Moor

For more details visit our website at
http://www.doctorwho.co.uk